Mille Basia 3

part 2

Contents

A few words from the author..8

Smells Like Scotland 12

Edinburgh Spectacular 14

Consumption 16

A Long Goodbye 18

Live Your Life...21

Walk With Me Brother 23

The Strength of a Woman..25

Contents of a Sporran 27

A Big Mistake 29

What Price My Freedom 31

Another Wife 33

A Lost Soul...35

Purely a Matter of Business..37

Unfinished Business..39

Bearing a Grudge..41

Joans Thoughts 43

The Grief of Parting 45

Across an Ocean...47

Dazed and Confused..50

A Letter to America...52

Lost With All Hands...54

The End of My World...56

Arch Bugs Revenge 58

Inconvenient Proposal 61

Touché Madam! 63

Arrivals and Departures 66

Being Willie. 68

A Wild Goose Chase...71

Lost over Scotland 72

Deadpan...74

On Your Feet soldier..76

Warmer/Colder 78

Feelings In Check 79

Until Death 81

She Will Not Grieve Alone......................................83

Carnal Knowledge 85

Shall We Dance 87

Consternation..89

Clearing the Air...91

Lashing Out...94

The Burning Question...95

A Simple Service 97

Let The Spirit Move You! 99

Poor Lord John..101

Have We Met Before Sir? 103

Refugees 105

Shameful Behaviour.. 106

The Gift of Sleep 109

Did He?... 111

No Bed Involved 113

Potting Shed 115

Fine Dining 117

Thinking On Ones Feet.. 119

A Coat of Red (reprise) 121

Blue Is The Colour 123

Epicurean... 125

Three Hundred Men.. 127

The Void 129

Remembering 131

Ellen's Prayer 133

Sisters 135

Dirty Laundry 137

Confessions of a Whore....................................... 139

Leopards and Spots 141

Women at War 143

Eye Eye... 145

Spotswood 146

4

Truth and Reputation...148

I Killed a Man Today 150

Protection...151

Shot In The Dark 153

Back To The Future..154

Shotgun Wedding 156

Gut Feeling..158

Grudging Respect 159

Insufferable Woman...161

Hold Your Fire 163

Flint Locked 165

Gut Shot!..167

Resignation...169

Surgeons Skill..171

Penicillium Roqueforti..173

When Ye Were Not Watching..175

Unconscious Thoughts 177

Cloaked in Darkness 179

The Price of Faith 181

Kidney Function..183

Last Resort. 185

False Confession...187

Condemned 189

Stinking Papist 191

And One More Thing! 193

Soul Searching 195

Reunited 198

Ghosts of The Past 200

The Unlocked Door 202

Family Resemblance 204

Wolf Brother 206

A Lock of Hair...208

Tiddly Om Pom Pom... 209

A Bonnie Concubine 212

Pressing Business 214

The Perfect Woman..216

The Other Woman... 218

Quad Erat Demonstrandum................................. 219

Asthma Attack... 221

Held Hostage 223

Force of Nature..225

Mustard Plastered 227

Meeting as Friends 229

Fire... 231

Tragedy 233

Sophronia 236

I Spy...238

Invasion...240

Christmas Cleaning 243

Mince Pie Anyone? 245

A Magical Night 247

Danger! Sassenach at work.............249

Cooking Under Pressure 251

Situation Vacant..............................253

Fireside Thoughts 254

Window of Opportunity 256

After The Dishes..............................258

Do Not Disturb! 260

Contemplation 263

Hide And Seek! 266

New Years Morn..............................268

Merry Christmas Sassenachs 270

A Plan For All Season......................272

Copyright...275

Other work by the author................276

A few words from the author.

It was July 2007 and I was on my holidays on a Greek Island with my family when, having finished my poolside reading I came across the abandoned book pile in the hotel lobby.

Amongst the literary tomes and trashy romance novels, all bearing the scars of pool water and factor 15 sun protection I came across a book called Cross Stitch. I picked it up and read the back. It didn't exactly draw me in. It was however the best preserved of the books on offer and it at least appeared to have all its pages. Lots of them.

'That should last me for the rest of my hols.' I thought.

I tucked it under my arm and replaced its hole in the bookshelf with my finished novel by Phillipa Gregory.

Later that day, I returned Cross Stitch to the pile. I could not get past the first chapter. I retrieved my old copy of 'The White Queen' and decided to read it again rather than find a replacement.

Fast forward to 2019, Wales is in lockdown during the COVID19 pandemic. Whilst browsing Facebook and my TV channels and wondering if the internet was actively stalking me, I came across the Outlander TV Series. I fell in love with it. Not specifically with any character at first, but with the whole thing.

I became an addict, I joined a fan page on Facebook. Some of the more outrageous posts made me laugh. They painted vivid mental pictures of what went on in people's lives when they became hooked on a drama.

Pause:

I have always dabbled in poems and rhymes. Mainly bawdy verses to add to my colleagues retirement or birthday cards. One particular Christmas themed poem circa 1992 got me into heaps of trouble with the boss. Whilst sitting in my garden on that particularly sunny COVID summer, I started to write.

I posted a poem on the Facebook page.

Someone asked if I had written any more.

I hadn't......but I did.

Then I started to read the books again. This time, having ridden over the hump of the first few chapters I loved them. I think I read them all that summer.

Then there was the drought, the gap in production, the wait for the book called 'Go Tell the Bees I have Gone.' It became my challenge to post a new poem every morning. I started my own page lest some fans object to my work. I sought consent from Diana Gabaldon herself to use her work. I received an email from her PA giving the go ahead.

I decided to donate any revenue generated to Riding for The Disabled. (My local group where I volunteer and am training as a riding coach).

Now I have written and published over six hundred poems. All are inspired both by the TV Series and by the incredible books written by Diana Gabaldon.

Eventually I sat down and compiled these poems into a chronological series called Mille Basia.

As far as is possible (given the diversions the show sometimes takes and the immense detail in the books which is sometimes bypassed in the process.) I have followed the progress of the story as it was written and also how it has been adapted for screen.

Mille Basia vol 1: Follows the story from the start up until the Frasers leave Scotland on the search for young Ian.

Mille Basia Vol 2: Picks up the story in the colonies and will take you as far as the point where the MacKenzies have returned to Scotland with their children.

Mille Basia Vol 3: Part 1.: A book divided into two parts due to the split in season seven. It follows the Frasers through the trauma of Claires imprisonment and the downfall of the Browns. The sorry tale of Tom Christie and then to the end of Season 7. Part 1. Ends with the Frasers returning to Scotland.

This book *Mille Basia Vol 3. Part 2.* Picks up the story after the break in season 7 of the TV Series but also follows the story as it is written in the novels.

To assist with the timeline, I have tried to include one line of context where I have felt it will assist the reader. This volume will take us up to the end of Season 7.

Because of the detours made by the screenwriters, I have extracted some of the book inspired verses from the main flow of this volume and given them their own section. This happens when they relate to characters or situations which have been completely missed out of the TV series but who have inspired me to write. There are several.

I will end this foreword by giving a huge thank you to Diana Gabaldon. If she has ever read any of my work, I hope she has enjoyed it in a tongue in cheek manner. I have on occasion made the most of the humour of the books and also gone what I call 'Off Piste' to include a section called 'A Frasers Ridge Christmas.' Which plays on the humour which abides in the relationship between Jamie and Claire.

Diana Gabaldon I thank you for your work and for your gracious tolerance of mine. It may gratify you to think that you also inspired me to write a series of novels of my own (details at the rear).

Thank you too to the cast, crew and production team of Outlander the TV Series for continually surpassing themselves.

With the end of Season 7 in sight and Season 8 in the can will there be a Mille Basia 4?

Watch this space!

Smells Like Scotland

It's so close, I can smell it.
The scent of Scottish sea,
And Sam and Cait are over here,
They've been on the BBC.

The voyage is now over,
The ship will finally dock,
Jamie in his homeland.
Back to Lallybroch.

Best get your supplies in,
Buy your snack of choice,
Brush up on your Sky Boat song,
Make sure you're in good voice.

Do you have your tissues,
Is there a wee dram by your side,
I fear there may be heartbreak,
We are in for a rough ride.

Book the couch for Friday,
Keep tabs on the remote,
If your husband goes out for the night,
Make sure he takes his coat.

The lights are dimmed, the curtains closed,
Are you comfy in your nest,
Settled in your armchair
For the thing we love the best.

Fourteen months of waiting,
Kick your plans right to the kerb.
Hang that sign upon the door
PLEASE DO NOT DISTURB.

Without further ado......let Season 7 part 2 begin............

20th December 1777
The Frasers have arrived in Edinburgh

Edinburgh Spectacular

There's a woman looking at me,
She's dressed in brown and gold,
I think she's seen a lot of life,
But doesn't look that old,

Her hair is shot with silver,
It curls around her face,
Her skin is clear, her eyes are bright
Of war there's little trace.

The winter bitten hungered look
Of living on ones wits
Hasn't yet invaded her,
Or any of her bits,

Not dressed like a pauper,
Not suffering from lack
HM's Navy fed us well,
On the voyage back.

They suit ye lass, I hear him say
They're bonnie on yer face,
Accept ye needed spectacles,
I take this with good grace.

Sassenach, ye wear it well,
After all the times we've had,
A little tweaking here and there,
Ye din'nae scrub up bad.

Remorseless Scott, be quiet
Must you lower the tone,
I'm starting to enjoy the view,
Through these lenses of my own.

Looking in the mirror,
I haven't done in years,
I see him there behind me,
And I'd love to box his ears,

He sees me now through steel rimmed frames,
With rose tint in the glass,
He is not looking at my face,
His eyes are on my arse.

Sassenach you look beautiful,
Yer eyes now rimmed with gold,
Ladylike, distinguished,
And not any less bold!

I am no longer eagle eyed,
But even I can see
Yer beauty leap through every pore,
And ye've only eyes fer me.

Let's away tae Mowbray's,
Ye'll be needing a good feed,
Ye have nae met wee Andy Bell,
He's a spectacle indeed!

All is not well on the return to Lallybroch..........

Consumption

Was it fate that we arrived
To witness Ian's end,
His youngest son returning,
Along with his best friend.

The family all gathered,
He'd made his peace with life,
He said goodbye to each of them,
But not yet to his wife.

She found me in the barn yard,
She begged me heal her man
Tell me you can cure him Claire!
Her desperate words began.

Consumption is an evil
For which there is no cure,
A dreadful bleeding coughing death,
And death it is for sure.

The cough he caught in prison
Never left his chest
It ate his flesh, made him weak,
With time he was not blessed.

Then she called me vengeful,
Asked why I did not stay,
For all the hardship suffered
In the time I was away.

16

I'm a healer, not magician,
She does not understand.
There is no cure, no magic salve,
No potion at my hand.

She begs me for forgiveness,
Tells me of her plan,
To never lose her brother,
She must tie him to the land.

With me he'll always wander,
We have no settled home,
She knows now that we two are one,
He will never let me go.

Her husband is a good man,
Eternally a friend.
I'd cure him if there was a way.
On that she could depend.

I hope that we can make a peace,
And both of us forgive,
Let Ian know that we are friends
In the time he has to live.

For die he will, and then his soul,
Flies pain free to the light,
But always there on Jenny's left,
And guarding Jamie's right.

Ian Mor says goodbye......................

A Long Goodbye

I ken my life is ending,
Hello precedes goodbye,
Still tis fine tae see ye all,
Hush now, din'nae cry.

My lungs are raw as pounded meat,
They go tae join ma leg,
At least it will ha' company.
And me still walking wi' my peg.

Tis braw tae see the family,
I ken ye mean the best,
There's messages fer all of ye,
If I can cough them of ma chest!

Michael, listen well tae Claire,
She tells ye of wars drum.
In Paris lies great danger,
She sees what is tae come.

Jenny, find forgiveness,
I am beyond repair,
Claire loves ye like a sister, aye.
Tae scold her is'nae fair.

Dinnae fash now son of mine,
I ken yer heart is bound,
Dinnae leave the one ye love,
Caring fer yer hound!

Jamie, I have much tae say,
Let us take a walk
While my leg still holds me up,
And I've still breath to talk.

Take care of yer sister,
Ye ken she has tae grieve,
I shall always be with her,
Even should she leave.

Dinnae let her fade away,
A widow wearing weeds,
She needs a life apart from here,
You must plant those seeds.

And yes I'll keep yer finger,
And you 'll keep me in yer prayers,
I hope the Lord has kept ma limb
Or I won't make it up his stairs.

Ye'll have an easy time of it,
He's bound tae let you in!
Tis me he'll send tae purgatory,
You weren't a man tae sin.

For now, let's sit and bide a while,
While stars and moon shine bright,
My brother in eternity,
You always guard my right!

Ian Mor tells his youngest son to go and find the woman he loves.

Live Your Life

I can'nae keep her waiting,
Stringing her along,
My place is here, right by your side.
I've been away too long.

I write tae say I'm staying,
I send the note with Claire,
If Da must die, I'll no' see you
Fall into despair.

Mother din'nae say a word,
Don't destroy that note.
My mind is fixed, yer youngest son
Will nae catch the boat.

Listen son, you have a life,
Yer Da would have you live,
Happy with a family,
The joy that that can give.

He'd want tae see ye happy
If it's far across the sea,
Not staying out of duty,
Looking after me.

We placed a stone for Iseabail,
Somewhere to call her home,
We ken ye are a wanderer,
Ye'll never cease to roam.

Go and find your Rachel,
Go with all our love,
Find a heart that fits with yours,
Like hands fit in a glove.

As Claire must go to save a life,
You must go find yours,
Your father, he would want it so.
And Lallybroch endures.

My brother did'nae drag ye back,
Ye came home out of love.
Now go with all the blessings
Go find yer Quaker dove.

Ian Mor and Jamie Reminisce ....

Walk With Me Brother

One more nip tae ease the cough,
It stabs right through ma chest,
If death is close, she takes her time,
And gives me little rest..

Do ye remember how when we were lads,
We played amongst these hills,
With wooden swords we practiced,
Honing warrior skills.

Yer father taught us tactics,
To parry, thrust and wheel
Guard each other's weaker side,
Or feel the kiss of steel.

Aye! Twas you that offered friendship
After Willie died
Ye claimed me as a brother,
A blood oath made with pride.

We made yer father wield the strap,
ran wild across the heather,
Being boys our exploits always
end in stripes of leather.

Dinnae laugh, too hard now,
I'll have Jenny on ma case,
If you go home wi' one less lung,
And blood upon yer face.

Just one more nip of whisky,
Jamie, din nae make me cry
Blood brothers in eternity,
I am not scared tae die.

Here's to you my loyal friend,
Ian, pass the flask,
If we came here to say goodbye
I'm not up to that task.

We'd best be gone, the sun is low,
There's darkness on the hill,
With kin ye love on either side,
Go now if ye will.

Departing soul, fly on the mist,
'Tis time tae end life's fight
Me and Jenny see ye safe,
And headed for the light.

Jenny Mourns her husband...............

The Strength of a Woman.

A plaintive piercing screaming,
Rings around the wood,
Venting pain and anguish,
Un noticed if she could.

Sister should I leave ye,
Alone tae voice yer grief,
Or do ye need yer brothers arms,
Is my comfort some relief?

How shall I live without him,
How shall I carry on?
How will I live life a widow?
My heart and soul all gone.

Twas you held us together,
You fed us with your love,
You cooked and cleaned, became our Ma
When the Lord took her above.

Twas you who watched our father die,
Twas you who saved my life,
Who faced down raiding redcoats,
Was mother, yes and wife.

Bairns ye've birthed and buried,
This ground has seen it all.
You are the glue which binds us.
Ye've seen us through it all.

Unspoken words plain on her face,
This death will be too hard
This grief may be the final stone,
Which breaks her strong façade.

He is blind, can't see her crumble,
Watch her foundations rock,
Ian's death the catalyst,
Will she leave Lallybroch?

Contents of a Sporran

Odds and ends of everything
All will have a use,
That or some deep meaning,
The owner is obtuse,

Bits of string, and fishing line,
A piece of cork with hooks,
A moles foot – 'gainst rheumatics ken!,
Some stones and one small book.

A Bible, from Fort William,
When he was first flogged,
Belonging to another boy,
Whose life was also dogged.

Things to use in times of need,
He said he'd keep me fed,
We may not have much else to use,
Save heather for a bed.

This was what he promised
All those years ago,
A long way now from Scotland,
I know it is still so.

And if I'm peely wally,
He surely has a cure,
A twist of this will see me right,
He smiles and says he's sure.

And daytime ghosts can soon be laid
Their haunt brought to a halt,
A sprinkling of his magic dust,
I think I call it salt!

Protective of its contents,
Some items are quite foreign,
His amputated finger?
He keeps that in his sporran.

Now Sassenach it could be worse
Can I bring ye to a halt?
Young Ian still has Forbes's ear,
Preserved in his, with salt!

Jamie reflects on the day he married Laoghaire!

A Big Mistake

My old room, from a wee small boy,
A day remembered well,
My wedding day to Laoghaire
The match was made in hell.

Reflection in the water,
My face and thoughts askew,
With each scrape of the razor,
A stranger came to view

A new shirt sewn together,
From all that we could find,
The preacher waiting patient,
Panic in my mind.

To be part of a family,
To find myself a place,
Find some happiness and peace,
The past try to erase.

I'd felt a stirring in ma kilt,
That's one worry eased,
At the thought of bedding,
Ma cock at least was pleased.

Second thoughts were banished,
I could nae let them down,
So, Ian walked me to my fate,
And vows made with a frown.

29

Twas wrong of me to do it,
I could nae give her love,
Ma mind was never with her,
It was with you my dove.

She did 'nae want my pity,
She thought she held my heart,
Or at least I needed her,
She thought that from the start,

Days of tears and silence,
One long domestic frost,
No laughter on the menu,
No zest in life the cost..

Marsali and Joannie
My only joy in life
I was the Da they never had
But I did'nae need a wife.

Laoghaire Mackenzie,
How many years must pass,
I was married to a woman,
You will always be a lass!

Your fetch was at the altar Claire,
Your ghost lay in our bed,
Twas only you could heal me,
She could only wish ye dead.

Joan needs a quiet chat with Da!

What Price My Freedom

A slow walk through the woodland
Away from flapping ears,
Joannie has a problem,
To Da she pours her fears.

Ma would have me married,
I would be wed to God.
Da, you do not think it strange.
Ma thinks me quite odd!

She will na send ma dowery,
She says she's found a man.
She will nae wed her own good self,
That is nae in her plan.

She kens that if she marries
She loses what she gets,
She wants the penny and the bun.
Now she's hedging bets.

A deal is forged on paper,
Balriggan is the price,
Two golden shots, for her and him.
That should break the ice.

Ned still knows his contracts,
Still sprightly, with no teeth
A signature is all it needs,
We all sigh with relief.

Mackenzie's are all schemers,
The Frasers stubborn men.
A lethal combination,
To bargain with, ye ken.

Free at last from Laoghaire,
Young Joan may think twice,
If her vocation is behind a veil.
He will gladly pay the price.

Claire recalls another meeting with Laoghaire

Another Wife

He's trying to tell me something,
He cannot find the way,
He sidesteps and prevaricates,
Is it going to take all day,

The atmosphere is wanting,
I sense there's something wrong,
They're hardly pleased to see me,
I smell a rat, and strong!

Privacy a premium,
He starts again to tell,
Stumbles for the words to say
He's in some personal hell.

A child's expectant entrance,
Joy upon her face,
Followed by her sister
Is it me who is out of place

Daddy! her first greeting
Goes through my soul like ice.
My heart fell through my stomach,
My insides in a vice.

And here she comes hard on their heels,
Spluttering for breath,
Red faced, angry, stuttering
The one who wished me death.

Her eyes meet mine across the room
I see her face grow paler,
Then it all comes tumbling out
In language of a sailor.

Confused, he sent her packing
She stumbled through the door
'My husband now' her parting words
She hated me for sure.

To stand my ground or run away
My heart feels only chills
My mind tells me to pack my bags
And high tail for the hills

A price agreed, a hasty deal,
Anything for peace,
To rid him of her shackles,
But there was scant release.

For years he held that burden,
In guilt, and cold hard gold,
And now he seeks forgiveness,
In faith, it leaves me cold.

Again, she'll take his money,
For she will never have his love,
God give me strength to understand,
And guidance from above!

More reflections on the subject from Jamie.

A Lost Soul

Going through the motions,
For all those missing years,
Decisions made without a thought
For other people's fears.

Lacking in emotion,
Not caring if I died,
Survival shows the worst in men
I've cheated and I've lied.

Ye see my finger tapping,
Ye ken all of my tells,
You know just what I'm thinking,
Tis one of yer spells.

Decisions that I would ha made,
Are harder now with you,
I've not just me tae think of,
It's a consequence for two.

Like spring has come into my life,
Returning to dead ground,
Feelings lost in years of frost,
Are waiting to be found.

Green leaves of hope are sprouting,
Flowers of joy will bloom,
That light that shines into my heart,
When you light up my room.

Yesterday I'd nothing
Except to carry on,
Today I've a whole life to live,
Tis you that brought the sun.

Joy and hope, oh yes and fear,
Rush in and I must choose,
Yesterday I'd nothing
Now I've so much more tae lose.

Jamie goes visiting!

Purely a Matter of Business

A raft of rare emotions,
Buried in the ground,
I stood upon the highland turf
While storm clouds brewed all round.

The storm is of my making,
The seeds sown years ago.
Coming home, they germinate.
I fear this storm will grow.

Home is where you leave things,
The place that knows your truth,
A place you faced your darkest hours,
And the place you left your youth.

The place to which your soul returns,
And of things you wish best dead,
Acts which always plague you,
Mistakes which haunt your head.

The happy, sad reunion
Picking up the thread.
Walls so full of memories,
Of the living and the dead.

37

Things must be concluded,
Or our lives somehow diminished,
I can'nae sleep well in ma bed
Wi' business left unfinished.

Cards laid on the table,
Honesty prevails.
Once again I lose my wife
As cross the sea she sails.

Unfinished Business

Balriggan is a lovely spot,
A calm and tranquil place,
Why did I choose to go there?
Just to show my face,

Maybe curiosity,
I knew she had a man,
Maybe to apologise,
Was that part of my plan?

Mistakes I made when I was young,
I should have told her then,
I never was in love with her,
Men played with her ye ken.

I never would have married her,
She was too young and bold as brass,
She'd never live the life I'd lead,
She'll always be a lass!

Jenny wanted happiness,
With me right by her side,
The only way she'd have it,
Was if I took a bride.

I tried my best to please them all,
With the part of me war left,
Most of me was far away,
Desolate, bereft.

She has nae changed her attitude,
She will not even listen,
Still blames me for all her ills,
If she had a brain it's missin'.

She will nae marry Joey,
She'd rather live in sin.
Then I have to keep her,
And she's money coming in.

I've said that I am sorry,
I can'nae say much more,
Then I'm dodging flower pots
And fighting on the floor,

I'll let the water of the Loch
Calm me of this care,
I've washed Laoghaire Mackenzie
Right out of my hair.

Bearing a Grudge

Ye owe me Jamie Fraser!
I knew ye should be mine,
She stole ye with her English charms,
Her eyes like well-aged wine

Ye owe me for those kisses
Stolen from my heart,
I was only light relief,
My feelings torn apart,

Ye owe me for my waiting,
For aye – I waited years,
Two marriages, two children,
And Tis you that they love dear

Ye owe me for that marriage,
That day I thought I'd won,
You were the prize I wanted,
But my pain had just begun.

Ye owe me something like the truth,
Recall the day we wed,
She stood there at the altar,
Lay in our marriage bed.

Ye come here to say sorry,
Ye come to make amends,
I don't forgive, I won't forget!
We never will be friends.

For you owe me a living,
And I will have my way,
I'll live upon the pound 'o flesh
your conscience makes ye pay!

Ye come here in yer finery,
To pay me with yer gold,
A lassie not a woman – aye!
At least I am not old!

Yer welcome to yer ancient witch,
But you'll pay to be set free.
I once loved ye Jamie Fraser
But ye never needed me!

Joans Thoughts

She brought a Da into our lives,
He loved us as his own,
Promised to look after us,
Until we were full grown,

But Ma has troubles in her mind,
She can'nae see her way,
Her weeping and her wailing
Will not make him stay.

Her mind is dwelling in the past,
And she cannot forgive,
When he went with that Sassenach,
That Witch should never live.

And now she's married half the man,
For Da is always sad,
He loves us dear but longs for her,
And the life that he once had.

He cannot make her happy,
Jealousy consumes,
That Witch she sees is always there,
Hiding in the room.

She will use his name and status,
She'll make him send her gold,
She says he's hers and she won't part,
Until her grave be cold.

In truth, he tried, it couldn't work,
For he was never free,
They meet each other through all time,
The English Witch and he.

I've ne'er seen Ma so angry,
The Witch back from the dead,
Ma was called to Lallybroch
And found them both in bed.

Ma could not fight the love they have,
Not with an ill wish charm,
Deranged and jealous took his gun,
She shot him in the arm.

She never will forgive him,
Though she has other men,
She will take his money,
That's all she wants I ken.

Gold ointment for my mother's soul,
When there was but one cure,
Claire heals his mind and salves his wounds,
She's not a witch I'm sure.

Now Da is truly happy,
Though he is far away,
I keep him safe inside my heart,
And for him I will pray.

20th March 1778

The Grief of Parting

I think tae weep ye need tae feel
All I feel is numb,
I sit here looking at the door,
I wait fer ye tae come,

I ken that now ye have nae pain
Yer in a better place,
Still, I sit and look fer you,
I can'nae see yer face.

Yer chair is ever empty,
Ma bed tis halfways cold,
I never thought tae be like this,
And not sae very old.

Ye bore it all wi patience,
Wi humour dry as bone,
While coughing tore yer lungs apart,
And dried ye up like stone.

The lord says that I must forgive,
I can'nae do that yet,
And the cruelty of the English,
I never shall forget.

No longer is this place ma home,
'Tis time for me tae leave,
I shall go wi ma brother then,
Will ye tell me not tae grieve,

Jamie says ye are with him
Always to his right,
So, on my other side ye'll lie.
When I sleep at night.

I have nae wept, I can'nae feel
I think 'tis called bereft,
My heart is empty as a shell,
Whose owner up and left

Ian if yer listening,
I ken I talk tae much,
I shall always have ye wi' me,
And hunger for yer touch.

Yer Will is read, all debts are paid,
All things handed on,
My bags are packed, ma brother waits
'Tis time that I was gone.

Before I rise, there's just one thing,
Tis preying on ma mind,
If yer body lies in Scotland
Should I leave yer leg behind!

Across an Ocean

Staring out across the waves
Leaning on the rail,
Heaving deck beneath ma feet,
I'm just a little pale.

Goodbye again tae Scotland
My homeland steeped in blood
My sister now has no ties there,
Are we leaving her for good,

Sassenach I hear you call,
From far across the sea,
Ye sound all fashed and in distress,
Yer face I can'nae see

I hear yer soul in torment,
I feel ye call of pain,
The words are lost in howling wind
And sheets of driving rain.

Sassenach I'm coming home
Hold on tae that thought,
Invisible the binding thread
Across an ocean, taught.

As long as I can hear ye,
And as long as I'm afloat,
Ye will na lose me to the waves,
Ifrinn I hate this boat!

I hear yer cries of anguish
Yer thoughts tae take yer life
Have faith in what yer soul can feel,
That holds ye as my wife,

We did nae board Euterpe,
It was not us that sank,
Fate said we should miss that tide,
We have God tae thank

Wait in safety, wait in peace,
No need for ye tae fash
Calm yerself and keep the faith,
We'll no have a strammash

Hold on tight to all we vowed,
Bind yer thoughts to me,
Sassenach I will be home,
Just not in time for tea.

Meanwhile
in another time
Maybe 1739!

Roger and Buck search for Jemmy
Rogers internal monologue is in italics

Dazed and Confused

You act as if you know me sir,
Or is that just your way,
How can I help your ailing friend,
To help ye on yer way?

She arched a knowing eyebrow,
My heart sank, fit tae die,
I thought she saw just what I was,
In the twinkle of her eye.

Talking round in circles,
Evading every truth
Geillis must see who I am,
She saw me in my youth.

She goes to make a potion,
Foxglove for Bucks heart,
Has Coincidence or fates design,
Made her play her part.

She has killed several husbands,
Please try not tae flirt,
Just sit and drink yer foxglove tea,
Buck, try and stay alert.

50

Now Buck that is yer mother,
Should we be in this time?
And here's yer bloody father,
Is adultery a crime?

These times are so confusing,
My thoughts best in my head,
Is Jamie's uncle Dougal
Really taking her tae bed!

A charm took from the faerie man,
Oh God! I need a beer
My father's dog tags in my hand!
That must be why we're here!

Meanwhile Jamie writes to Claire of his stopover in France

A Letter to America

The writer writes with Quill and ink
On parchment stiff and old,
A friend is gone, his end is come,
His body has grown cold.

A stilted hand, aches with time,
It crawls across the page,
Tears flow, the ink will run,
With sadness, not with rage.

He writes across the endless sea,
He writes to one who waits,
He writes to ease the endless ache,
The loss of Ian creates.

He writes of telling stories
Told to pass the time,
A raconteur of talent,
Discoursing in his prime,

He worries for his sister,
Her grief is inward turned,
Living now within her shell
Her outer layers burned.

He tells her they will start for home,
They leave the shores of France,
Passage booked on the Euterpe
And so, begins a dance.

52

He yearns to lie beside her,
To feel her touch, anon
Sorrow writes the final page,
The ink stained wretch signs off!

Lost With All Hands

A visitor in blue and braid,
Lord John in distress,
What is wrong, I am confused.
And worried I confess.

Lost.... all hands
I hear the words
Sunk without a trace
They echo, but they do not stick,
The truth writ on Johns face.

Lost .....all hands
I hear again.
Claire, I fear him dead,
Lost at sea, the ship is sunk
Chaos fills my head.

All hands lost.... survivors. None.
Taken by a wave.
They stayed to search, but all in vain
There was no one to save.

He is not dead, I am alive.
My fighting heart reacts,
If he were dead, I would have died,
I rail against the facts.

Lost all hands...do you not see
The Captain saw it all,
A freak wave in a violent storm,
Not just an April squall.

If he were dead, my heart would stop,
Our hearts are truly tied
It is not so.... I know he lives.
I will not be denied.

The Captain came straight from the dock,
He did not come in jest,
A name on paper is his proof.
That is manifest.

Tears of grief rolled down our cheeks,
Tears of two, bereft,
Tears for what we both had lost,
We cried till none were left.

The man who loved what he could not touch,
And I who gave my soul,
All petty jealousy aside,
We will keep each other whole.

The End of My World

He is dead!
The world stopped turning!
I wasn't in control,
Surely, I would feel him missing,
Somewhere in my soul.

Drowned!
There is no coming back,
If he is lost at sea,
Surely there is some mistake,
I still feel him with me!

Lost!
I sit and watch the door,
But he will not come home,
This time, is he really gone,
Am I on my own

Grief!
Is such a little word,
For a feeling oh so large,
It occupies the whole of you,
With misery in charge.

Choices!
I think through all the methods
And the poisons, in my head.
What's the most effective way,
To render myself dead.

Comfort!
Pour the brandy,
I shall drink until I'm numb,
Deaden all my senses,
Surely sleep will come.

Company!
But I am not the only soul,
Who mourns his death alone,
Bring another bottle John.
Don't drink on your own!!

Arch Bug knows how to bear a grudge like a true Scotsman.

Arch Bugs Revenge

What is it friend? I asked his dog,
What smells are in your head
His nostrils sniffed around my feet,
I bartered for the bread.

Then he was off, upon the scent,
He would not be distracted,
No obstacle could bar his way,
Attention was attracted.

I cursed that dog, you hound of hell
What is it that you track,
Not squirrel, no! nor rabbit,
Could it be Ian back!

Sounds of voices, soldiers,
The chink of spurs and swords.
Rollo not distracted.
His goal he moves towards

A white haired man, with half a hand,
He walked upon a stick,
Was watching from the shadows,
His movement old, but quick.

A grip of iron grabs me,
His eyes bore into mine,
Ye love Ian Murray!
A statement – of my crime!

I see the axe hung on his belt!
He surely means me harm
I scream! Someone must hear me
Raising the alarm

A soldier running headlong
Charges him for sure,
The axe blade strikes,
And William lies unconscious on the floor.

Arch Bug will try for vengeance
Until he's lying cold
Ian's love will pay with life,
Before Arch grows too old.

And Rollo has found Ian,
Just as things were getting nasty,
Reunited just as he
Had stopped to buy a pasty.

William scraped up off the ground,
Is now confined to bed,
Wounded pride, a dented skull
Claire's stitches in his head.

Arch is now a fugitive,
A price upon his head,
A stramash in the print shop
Just might see him dead!

Vengeance, now in front of him,
Then all became a blur,
Arch is taken to the floor
A mass of teeth and fur

59

Axe in hand he lashes out
And Ian's arm he hooks
Saves his wolf and takes the blow,
And Rachel throwing books.

Blood and fur and teeth and Ian
Roiling on the floor,
Tall and lean and gallant,
He barged in through the door

Into the fray a soldier,
in a coat of red
Why you and men with axes friend!
His pistol shoots Arch dead!

Claire has been spotted running messages for the rebels and is about to be arrested........

Inconvenient Proposal

I'm not a fan of Richardson,
He is a turkey cock,
What face does he wear today
More than the Town Hall clock,

I've a sadness tearing out my heart,
He intrudes upon my grief,
I fear he does not come in peace,
There is truly no relief.

How well do I know her?
This widow of a friend,
He is seeking information,
But what does he intend?

Claire! what were you thinking,
You, stupid, headstrong fool!
Spying for the rebels,
Whilst under British rule.

For the love I bear your husband,
For the love he bore for you
To save you from the hangman,
There's but one thing I can do.

61

Claire Fraser! You will marry me?
Like tumbleweed in dust,
The words fall soft on deafened ears..
Hear me Claire, you must!

He plays his cards close to his chest,
He has evidence in spades.
Letters left, sedition writ.
This cannot be delayed.

It's all that I can offer,
The best that I can do,
They will not take my family,
That family must be you.

It's not just you he'll come for,
But all those in your life.
For Jamie's kin, to save their necks.
You MUST become my wife.

A marriage inconvenient,
We must declare a truce,
I loved a man, and he has gone.
Let that love have some use.

Claire, put aside your anger,
This is not time to make a stand.
For the love we share for Jamie,
Take my offered hand.

Lord John is a bit of a bigot! He and Claire have an argument.

Touché Madam!

Henry would marry Mercy,
The woman he adores,
To hell with what his father thinks,
To hell with social mores.

He would forfeit all his titles,
It would be against the law,
Lords John shakes with anger,
It seeps from every pore!

Henry do not play the fool,
Your recovery is complete,
You will take the next boat home,
Now you're back upon your feet.

We argued in the carriage home,
The atmosphere fraught
I called Lord John a bigot,
He told me what he thought.

It is not Mercy's status
Or the colour of her skin,
Such marriage is against the law,
A punishable sin.

She is the widow of a traitor,
We are in times of war,
He would be disinherited,
That would be for sure.

Would you have him live his life
Lonely, just like you,
Alone for want of someone,
Whose love he knows is true

And when it comes to traitors wives,
To a pot the kettles black,
What am I, but a traitors wife.
Now can you answer back?

Madam you forget yourself,
Is your argument now done.
I am just Hal's brother,
Henry is his son!

I have lived a life of fear.
My very nature is a crime
Fear of discovery
Haunts me for all time.

Would you wish them persecuted,
Have them live outside the law,
Hunted down as animals
You surely know that score!

You may call me many things
bigot I am not.
Over Hal's dead body
Will they tie the knot!

Jamie returns...

Arrivals and Departures

Some men make an impact
Even when they're dead,
Or not dead, as the case may be,
hold on to that thread.

He could not come back quietly,
And he'd never comprehend
That His wife was now his widow,
And was wedded to his friend.

Barging in at Chestnut Street,
He's come to claim his wife!
One warm embrace then off again
Running for his life.

Eye to eye with William,
Who now twigged he was his son,
And redcoats banging on the door,
What has that Scotsman done?

A stand off on the landing,
Holds a gun on Lord John Grey.
Then they climb out of the window
When will he be back to stay?

And I am left explaining,
Picking up the pieces
Of a William in crisis,
I must include this in my thesis.

66

So, I am a bastard!
my father is a Scot.
All those things I thought I was,
I now know I am not.

He's a criminal, a traitor,
A Jacobite, a groom.
A filthy stinking papist!
Then William left the room.

Losing all composure
Fraser temper fully loaded,
The young 9th Earl of Ellesmere
Finally exploded.

The lovely house at Chestnut Street
No longer has a door,
The chandelier crystals
Are smashed upon the floor.

The bannisters are broken,
The panelling is trashed,
Exit stage left William
The cause of the strammash

And waiting on the doorstep,
Like the perennial bad penny
Quarrels all forgotten now,
Is Jamies sister Jenny!

She calmly raised an eyebrow
Willie charged out through the door
The son is like his father then.
She didn't have to say much more!

Being Willie.

My brain feels like it's going to burst,
Seems everyone but me,
Knew just who my real father is
And my family history.

My mother, well I knew she died,
Just as I was born
They told me she was headstrong,
treated everyone with scorn.

My father, 8th Earl Ellesmere.
I bear his name for sure,
But twas he who called me bastard,
And called my mother whore.

Grandmama and Grandpapa
Did their level best,
To hide from me the awful truth
Well-known to the rest.

Lord John and Isabel, my aunt
Raised me from a child
Taught me how to be an Earl,
Stopped me from running wild.

Why do I remember then
The happiest times to be
the stables at Helwater
Mac the groom and me,

He taught me how to love the land
He taught me how to ride
Taught me to swear in Gaelic!
I repeated it with pride!!

I was like his shadow
Until the awful day
Mac packed up his belongings
My hero rode away.

I cried for him for days and days
I wished him to come back,
I didn't think I'd see again
The groom they all called Mac.

I started hearing rumours
It wasn't very pleasant,
People started to remark
I don't look like my parents.

Mac was not his real name
He came to us from prison
Now he was in the colonies,
How were his fortunes risen.

I have his height, I have his build
I have his steel blue gaze.
His cheekbones and his sloping nose,
Looks I cannot erase.

The dawn of recognition,
Cut me like a razor,
When I look into the glass
I'm shaving Colonel Fraser.

Did he rape my mother,
Or was she just a whore?
Sleeping with the servants
Or is there something more.

He claims responsibility
For the fact she died,
He won't speak any ill of her.
He'll not say more – he lied.

Pride won't let me speak to him,
Nor the hurt that I remember
And the other thing I have from him
Is a red hot Fraser temper.

In Scotland in 1739 Roger and Buck are still searching for
Jem............

A Wild Goose Chase

Buck and I have searched in vain,
Of Jem there is no trace,
Half the highland folk alert,
Should they see his face.

A sighting of a Faerie man,
Wandering the moor
Does he have knowledge of my son,
We really can't be sure.

What guided us to find this place,
To place us in this time,
I thought of Jem to get us here,
Is this how the fates conspire.

Now I'm searching for my father,
The faerie man for sure,
Did he just fly back through time,
Not go missing in the war.

Is all this leading somewhere,
Will it lead to some release,
Are we travelling in circles,
Are we chasing wild geese!

71

Jerry Mackenzie is having an unfortunate experience...............

Lost over Scotland

One minute I was flying
But I was in control,
Testing out equipment,
Yaw and pitch and roll.

The moors of northern England
The world was at my feet,
The heathered hills of Scotland,
Tucked beneath my seat.

My compass loses function,
All points have lost their place,
Rolls Royce Merlin wizard,
Get me safely from this place.

The crash was hard, the ground was soft,
How did I survive,
I am where my plane is not!
At least I think I am alive.

The locals are suspicious.
I am a wanderer, but from when.
They think I am a traveller,
A faerie man ye ken!

Time has lost its meaning,
Now there's two men on my track,
Would they rob me of my future,
No, they want to send me back.

What does he try to tell me?
Have we met before?
He talks in riddles of his life,
He knows me that is sure.

Then the world turned upside down,
I'm flying once again
Lost in action, feared dead.
This time without a plane.

Meanwhile back in 1980 Brianna faces problems of her own............

Deadpan

Waiting, endless waiting
Exhaustion, loss and fear,
Half my family missing,
In what time, I've no idea!.

What has Cameron done with Jemmy,
He will not do him harm,
Jem knows where the gold is hid,
Maybe no cause for alarm.

A figure in my kitchen,
Gives me quite a shock,
Where is my son, how dare you!
Intrude on Lallybroch.

So, Jemmy would not tell you,
You sent him through those stones,
And now he's wandering lost in time,
Frightened and alone!

Yer husbands gone tae find him,
He's well out of the way,
There's no one left tae help ye hen!
I'm the boss today.

I have him safely hidden,
But he will not talk to me!
Did you really think he would?
You b**tard set him free.

Hen! pour a glass of red for me,
We've things we must discuss,
We'll take a flight, find the gold,
Just the three of us.

This man has bad intentions,
it is me he came to see,
No one will repeat the thing
Bonnet did to me!

The heavy orange saucepan,
Leaps into my hand,
Brandished like a broadsword,
a warrior guides my hand.

Give me strength to fight him!
I am not beaten yet.
Oops! there he lies! unconscious!
Thank you 'le Creuset

For the uninitiated Le Creuset is a make of very heavy cast Iron
cookware!

Jemmy finds a way out........

On Your Feet soldier.

Water, cold and darkness,
A prison without light.
No one here to help him,
Outside only night.

On your feet soldier,
Granny used to say,
Use your inner senses
You can find a way.

On your feet soldier,
Your mother was here too.
Remember everything she said,
Let her words guide you.

On your feet soldier,
It's like walking in the park
Find the switches, trip the lights,
Look! It's no longer dark.

On your feet soldier,
Somewhere the tunnel forks,
Take the right, but take good care.
It's not a pleasant walk.

Beware of the portal
It will try and drag you through,
Stay away, do not go near,
Whatever else you do.

You may hear voices calling,
From two hundred years away,
Do not listen to their call.
From your mission do not stray.

There is another doorway,
On the other side,
On your way now soldier,
Make your granny glow with pride.

Mandy and Bree play a game.........with a purpose

Warmer/Colder

Mandy can you feel him,
Tell me warm or not,
As we drive please think of him,
Are we getting hot!

Warmer,
As we cross the moors,
Colder, has he gone,
Colder still, he's truly lost,
The search goes on and on.

Colder,
Let's retrace our steps,
He's hidden in our time
What has that bastard Cameron done,
Kidnap is a crime.

Warmer,
Mummy warmer, Mummy boiling hot,
Mummy he is back.
Mummy, mummy stop the car
That's Jemmy on the track!

Back in Philadelphia Lord John grieves for his friend.............

Feelings In Check

I'm staring at a chessboard,
The pieces do not stir,
For all is not in black and white,
Life is now a blur!

My glass is nearly empty
Tis my last port in a storm,
Tears of loss and emptiness
Becoming quite the norm.

What I would give for one more game,
That meeting of two minds,
Cerebral ballet acted out.
The pleasure friendship finds.

My knight has fallen from his horse,
My king has met his fate,
Your rook is lost to all but grief,
Your queen pines for her mate.

It breaks my heart to hear her,
Fighting with her fears,
I know the loneliness she feels,
It has burdened me for years

My tears fall just as free as hers,
My feelings have not flown.
I know she cannot love me,
But she can't face this alone,

Is it wrong to find some comfort,
Is it sin to find release,
That memory of a mutual love
Should bring a scrap of peace.

For she was not a lady,
nor I a gentle man,
It was not an act of love,
Nor was it a plan.

A battle over common ground,
We f***ed as humans do!
Our feelings vented in the dust,
Our bodies bound to you!

Claire reflects considers ending her life. Did a voice from afar stop her?

Until Death

Another time another place,
Such a different groom,
Another marriage of convenience,
But one where love would bloom.

Another priest of different hue,
My thoughts were all astray
I Repeated like a wind-up toy
Love, honour, and obey.

Not my voice, I spoke the words
For better or for worse,
A ring, in sickness and in health,
A vow, or yet a curse.

John in all his finery,
Galant from the start,
Two players in a marriage farce,
Until death do us part.

I heard a voice, an echo.
Carried through the mist,
Calling from a watery grave,
My hearts knife gave a twist.

Death will never part us,
It will our souls unite,
If I should die, to be with you.
would my death be right?

Words that echoed in my mind,
Pronounce us man and wife,
I've poisons stocked in plenty,
Is it sin to end my life?

Is this a blade before me?
A blade forged just to heal,
That blade won't harm its owner,
Your voice cuts me, like steel.

Bone of my bone, I hear you.
Blood of my beating heart.
My living hell must be endured,
Our souls be torn apart.

Screaming, wrenching, tearing grief,
Heart heavy as a stone,
Your ocean in my bottle,
My heart must drown alone.

She Will Not Grieve Alone

Once more you were inside me,
I anchored to that point,
But you were dead, it could not be.
All feelings out of joint.

Skin on skin, breath mixed with mine,
It was you I felt,
The only way to play my cards,
This hand I had been dealt.

It started on the table,
It ended on the floor,
Baser feeling gratified
Behind a well closed door.

The reality of morning,
Some post coital facts,
How do you live with loneliness,
The awkward silence cracked.

He told me of Manoke,
He told me of a deer,
A blessing with no ties attached,
On that he was quite clear.

This man had lived a life alone,
His love against the law,
Resigned, or happy in his skin,
Of which I was not sure.

To know your whole life is a lie,
And on that to reflect,
This husband of convenience,
I view with new respect.

What couples do behind closed doors,
How people live their lives,
They act the part, behind a mask.
They hope they will survive.

Accept life's invitations,
Smile through gritted teeth.
The gliding swan, Lady John
Hides its turmoil underneath.

Carnal Knowledge

Accept some human comfort,
It may just ease the pain,
Until you venture from the dark
To join with life again.

Tis not your love I'm asking for,
I know your heart is taken,
Your mind is in another place,
If I am not mistaken.

Before you sacrifice yourself,
To live a life in chains,
At least remember how it feels,
I make no other claims.

Use it in the long dark nights,
Draw it to your mind
Keep some human feeling
Think of those you leave behind.

It's not unfaithful to her memory,
To keep your soul alive,
The memory of human touch,
May just help you to survive.

I heard the voice of Mary
Answering my prayer,
As I asked God to find a way
That I could forgive Claire.

Her love is very physical,
She thrives on human touch,
To grieve without that contact,
I would expect too much.

At least they have been honest,
And I did na lose my life,
Despite his Carnal Knowledge,
I love my errant wife.

Claire is forced to take part in polite society!

Shall We Dance

To dance is a distraction
With a partner you may find
A smooth coordination,
Of movement and of mind.

A grey man and a Lady,
Glide across the floor,
Moves upon life's chess board,
His motive, I'm not sure.

Richardson, the English spy,
A uniform of red.
Declares he is a rebel,
He would not see me dead.

This arch manipulator,
Thinks he has me in his palm,
Will I gather information,
Will I do my husband harm?

He has no sense of loyalty,
Eyes colder than a snake,
Betrayal not my middle name,
I'll not make that mistake.

I will not blow his cover,
We fight for the same side,
But spying on the house of Grey.
Sir! I have my pride!

William does not approve of Lord Johns marriage.

Consternation

Marriage to a rebel,
How can you hold your head,
Look your comrades in the eye,
Still wear a coat of red.

No more than a farmer,
He bore arms against the crown,
A groom, a pardoned traitor,
Papa do not frown.

Reputation, honour,
Do not take this amiss,
What degree of friendship
Would make you risk all this.

She cannot make you happy,
She won't fit with your life,
Her husband and her politics,
Not fitting in your wife.

I see that strange look in your eyes,
That one from far away,
Who was the man, what did he do?
Will you never tell me, pray?

A deep Scots voice outside the door,
He comes to find his wife,
Reunion, chased by redcoats,
He's been hunted all his life.

A brief exchange of kisses,
Soldiers on the stair,
Gazes locked across the landing.
Recognition in the glare.

Like looking in the mirror,
To Deny him, do not try.
Sir, I know well who you are,
But who the hell am I?

Ye are a stinking papist,
I chose tae call ye James,
Twas all that I could give ye,
Just one of ma names.

Papa! You kept it from me,
You knew it from the start
I want nothing from you,
Words to break a fathers heart,

How will Lord John break the news?

Clearing the Air

The pistol was not loaded,
I could see that, clear.
The soldiers running up the stairs
Saw the sense of the idea.

Yet again I am a pawn
In saving this man's life,
How then do I tell him
I have knowledge of his wife.

Red fox, always hunted,
Have you lost your charm,
That sense of danger so acute,
Alert to pending harm.

What sedition this time?
Playing fast and loose,
always walk outside the law,
Risk a traitors noose!

A flask, but only water filled,
For now, we speak as friends,
I fear my next announcement
May be where the friendship ends.

Din'nae look so worried John,
Ken yer sweating' and yer pale.
Is there aught that troubles ye,
Is yer heart about tae fail?

Yes, I will find Willie,
I shall try and mend his life,
And I think I'd better tell you,
Of my trouble and my strife wife.

Jamie, I would have you know,
Would you care to use a knife,
Kill me now, for I have
Carnal knowledge of your wife.

I was drunk and so was she,
We both believed you dead,
It was no act of married love,
We were f*cking you instead.

I felt my eye exploding,
I didn't see the fist.
A cloud of red, is that my blood,
Or a Fraser in red mist.

He tried to punch me once before,
Thought better of that act,
There are no chains to bind him now,
I will suffer for that fact.

A fist thrown with precision,
Eyes steel blue with rage,
My sight is gone, my ribs are broke.
God! Death can take an age!

Militia men intruding,
I have been recognised,
Play it canny, like a fox
Or we both get took for spies.

Meanwhile Claire picks up the pieces.... And the furniture!

Lashing Out

And I must cope with William,
a kettle on the boil,
A fuse lit, unexploded bomb,
An over tightened coil.

His questions must be answered
But who am I to tell,
Tis not my knowledge to disclose,
Oh! damn those men to hell!

One Fraser on the rampage,
The other on the run,
Obvious to all with eyes,
One is father, one is son.

Do I tell him of his mother,
Or should those truths be hid!
The lady who seduced the groom.
Would he believe me if I did!

The fuel that fires his feelings
I cannot assuage,
Lashing out with words and fists,
Blinkered in his rage.

Jamie is persistent with his questions!

The Burning Question

Ye feel the need tae tell me,
Ye had tae bed ma wife,
Now tell me all the truth of it,
Before I end yer life.

Tell me did ye b**ger her?
Explain tae me, please try?
I'm burning fit tae kill ye!
Dinnae think tae lie!

Ye ken I know yer preference,
The nature of the beast,
Before ye die, be honest,
I shall have the truth at least.

Is that why ye were worried,
You knew she'd tell me all,
I would deal with her in my own way,
So, you thought to take the fall?

Ye thought me dead,
Ye took her, she who holds my heart,
You thought to have yer way with me,
And she was just the start?

Ye wee perverted bastard,
There are no more words to say,
To f**k my wife, and think it me.
You will regret the day.

Ye'll go with the militia
They recognised ye aye.
With any luck, they'll have their way.
And hang ye as a spy!

In the books written by Diana Gabaldon the wedding of Ian and Rachel falls after the battle of Monmouth and before the return to the ridge.

A Simple Service

Like waiting for the dentist,
I din'nae mean tae mock!
The spirit surely takes its time,
It's nearly four o'clock.

A state of contemplation,
Until the time is right,
Sassenach this chair is hard,
Is it going tae tak all night!

Friend Jamie, do not whisper,
Pri' thee speak a words
It seems the spirit moves you,
Its time your voice was heard.

I am proud to own my nephew
And the man he's grown tae be
Since I held him in my arms crook,
When he was only wee!

Jamie, please keep quiet,
Maybe the spirit shouldn't say,
The things you put him up to,
Leading him astray!

The spirit moves the bride to speak,
She is happy with her life,
A simple act exchanging vows,
And now they're man and wife!

Let The Spirit Move You!

Let the spirit move you,
Say it as you feel,
Take the time to contemplate,
Let your spirit heal.

Plain speaking in the sight of god,
Do not be afraid,
Air your concerns frankly,
Before your vows are made.

No flowers, no fancy dresses,
No frippery, no frills
A borrowed frock well altered,
A bonnet hides her curls.

Sincerity, simplicity,
and Honesty they say,
You live a marriage for a life,
Not just for one day.

With kindness, understanding,
Negotiating skills,
Compromise may smooth a path
Through a clash of wills.

Let the spirit move them,
To the simplest of vows,
We all reflect on those we took,
With a wrinkling of brows.

Regrets we never mention,
Jealousies we feed,
Apologies we did not make,
And never saw the need.

Did the spirit move us,
Without the need for drink
In these moments of serenity.
We all took time to think.

Lord John is taken by the Rebel Militia!

Poor Lord John

My left eye closed and throbbing,
By Christ he throws a punch.
My head is sore from scalp to jaw,
I won't be chewing lunch.

The world is tilted sideways,
I feel slightly sick,
I couldn't feel much groggier
Had he hit me with a brick.

Look to the right - that's painful
Look to the left is worse,
Looking up won't happen,
It's enough to make one curse.

I'm talking utter garbage,
Yes! I took your wife to bed
Am I sorry! No, I'm not.
I was f***ing you instead.

You stupid Scottish bastard,
Kill me if you must,
The things we say in anger,
Or when just a bit concussed.

Escape before they hang me!
For a cousins evil raid.
Pay-o-Lee what the hell is that,
They would have that dept repaid.

God bless Denzel Hunter,
He supplied the knife,
God damn you Jamie Fraser,
And my knowledge of your wife.

Meanwhile Jamie has other business to attend to!

Have We Met Before Sir?

Welcome Colonel Fraser,
Have we met before?
Ah yes, it was in Wilmington,
That play was such a bore!

You carry letters from abroad,
You have not been waylaid?
Important correspondence.
Promises of aid.

Colonel Morgan sings your praise,
Your leadership of men,
Your bravery in battle,
Would you take up arms again?

Command of a battalion,
An elevated rank,
Brigadier General,
You have yourself to thank.

Flattering his ego,
In a Washingtonian drawl
Honeyed words of confidence
He will not resist the call!

He went in as a messenger,
He left, a Brigadier,
General Fraser has a ring!
And a uniform I fear!

Meanwhile the loyalists are leaving Philadelphia...................

Refugees

Wagon after wagon,
Each loaded up with life,
A families goods and chattels,
Topped off with a wife,

Some are pushing hand carts,
Belongings piled high,
The collected things that make up life
Pointing at the sky,

The threat of war, The sense of fear,
The City safe no longer,
Humanity is on the move,
Whose army will prove stronger?

The old, the young, the weak the strong,
The elderly and frail.
Rest along the dusty road,
Moving slowly up the trail.

They have no destination,
Their future is unknown.
Those with nothing surely die,
Before they find a home.

Like snails, their houses on their backs
A families whole life,
Furniture and belongings,
And on the top – a wife.

William is supervising the evacuation..............

Shameful Behaviour

An endless stream of human life,
Heading out of town
Following the army,
Loyal to the crown.

A friendly face, a Quaker lass,
Seemingly alone,
Rachel, object of his love,
In times which now have flown.

And he who called me kinsman!
Anger to the fore.
Cousin.... You... you knew it too.
My shame could not be more!

Yes, my uncle truly is your sire,
He is not what you assume.
He is a man of honour,
He was not just a groom.

Nose to nose, head to head,
Two stags in a rut,
I will never call him father,
He us just a heathen Scot.

106

Mohawk fights with Redcoat,
Grapple, hand to hand
You should be proud to share his blood,
There is no finer man.

Corporal seize this Indian,
Keep him well contained,
Fighting with an officer,
Rachel's wrath, inflamed.

You sir are a coward.
It is shame, what thee has done!
You struck first, thee goaded him.
Honour! Thee has none.

A lone dismounted horseman,
A warriors grip of steel,
A redcoat captain frogmarched
Wriggling like an eel.

Young man you will listen,
You will do as I say,
They will release your cousin
Before the close of day.

Chastisement of children,
Oft times must be done.
Underneath a roadside tree
A father chides a son.

Believe me when say to you,
I will tell the world,
exactly where you came from,
Your parentage unfurled.

What you did was shameful,
An act of utter spite,
Now go before I change ma mind,
Put the matter right.

The father gives a lesson,
He will discipline instil.
An old fox and a rooster.
a fiery clash of wills.

A redcoat and a rebel.
Two sides of one coin
General Fraser brings to book
The offspring of his loin.

William finds solace in a brothel and meets a very particular whore.

The Gift of Sleep

The finest gift to give a whore?
It is a good night's sleep.
A night of peaceful dormancy
Given the hours they keep.

I have met two Arabella's,
None that know your tricks
One of them is eighty two
The other one is six!

The madam says a fancy girl
Needs a fancy name
Twas she who bid me use it,
My real name is Jane.

Jane, I want nothing from you,
I have nothing left to give,
My life reduced to tatters
I have scarcely will to live!

No, I won't demand your service
Like the men who lounge downstairs,
Lewd in their discussion of
Sampling your wares.

My word is all I have to keep.
It will keep you for the night,
Sleep here in the armchair,
If that would be alright.

Sir, come to bed, pray join me.
For in the morning, you must go.
I will not molest you
If I offend, then tell me so.

A William in confusion
Finds refuge with a whore,
Some comfort in a strangers bed,
Sleep a gift for sure.

Meanwhile Jamie has caught up with Claire... The interrogation
continues......

Did He?

There are certain questions
Which you don't put into words,
You won't really like the answer
So, to ask is quite absurd.

Some things still, unspoken
Between a man and wife.
Too much information,
Can only lead to strife.

He feels the need to ask me,
The answer, I'll give none.
To the act of mutual comfort
I engaged upon with John

You would think I would remember,
That it would cut through the haze,
Be carved into my memory,
Never to erase.

He will not force an answer,
He knows I will not lie
What on earth has Lord John told him,
Do I need an alibi!

111

Strung tight as a bowstring,
Words as sharp as knives,
I'll not be interrogated,
Some of my pride survives.

I slap! my palm is stinging,
It deters him not one jot.
Was I thinking with my body?
I can't say I was not!

He tries with words of reason,
Compares his case with mine,
But the answer to his question
Remains lost, in brandy wine!

There are things he'll never tell me,
Things still hid behind his mask
Things he can't find words for,
Questions I no longer ask!

I will not feel guilty,
I will not feel shame,
We thought him dead, our feelings too.
Check mate, end of game!

No Bed Involved

He says ye went tae bed wi' him,
My insides quite dissolved,
No! I said succinctly,
There was no 'bed' involved.

It started on the furniture,
It ended on the floor,
cathartic and violent,
No love involved, I'm sure,

For days I'd sat and grieved for you,
Pondered my own death,
Listed ways to end my life,
Not take one more breath,

And he would have no more of it,
We both had lost a love,
One he was not entitled to,
As mine was, hand and glove,

There was a lot of brandy drunk,
With not a lot of care,
Both of us were joined in flesh
To a man who was not there,

That night we bared our mortal souls,
With you we both lay,
He with you, I not with him,
He's not my sort I'd say!

His arms were yours around me,
Your death left me forlorn,
His grief and mine carnally salved,
And shattered with the dawn.

And now you stand before me,
Demanding, with some gall,
I thought you dead my soul was lost,
John Grey saved me, that's all!

A scene they missed out in the TV series.

Potting Shed

She knelt there in the garden
Absorbed in herbs and weeds,
I'd questions boiling in my brain
And a wanting for man's needs.

I stood there waiting quietly,
I could ha' watched all day
Where the hell have you been?
Was all she had to say.

I smelt like hell and cabbages,
I had'nae washed in weeks
My brains had all migrated
They were hiding in ma breeks.

We sat and talked, I said my piece
Not as I had planned
The elephant of Lord John Grey
Was always there to hand.

I'd forgive her everything,
She is all my life,
I'd even forgive his lordship
Carnal knowledge of my wife.

Pandora's box was opened,
All its contents aired,
Cards upon the table,
No quarter has been spared.

115

To see her is tae want her,
I will find a spot,
Not in the grass where folk can hear,
Bed of flowers or not.

Bartram's brand new potting shed
Amongst the seedling plants,
I'd plant some seedlings of ma own
When remove these pants

I must have her naked,
I will make her beg,
At least I will when I can get
My breeks off down my leg

The storm broke all around us,
Thunder rolled in flesh
Lightening flashed between us
As two to one enmesh

I must have ye Sassenach
Remember you are mine
Hold that thought next time ye stray
And all will work out fine.

Be careful Jamie Fraser,
Insufferable Scott,
I'm still your wife, however
Obedient I am not.

In the series, however. The potting shed was substituted!!

Fine Dining

Claire I'm done wi' talking,
I have loved ye' all my life,
I can forgive ye most things,
Now are ye still my wife?

Thinking with yer body,
Leads to trouble every time,
What must I do to chastise you,
And keep ye off the brandy wine!

The servants are not present,
There is no one in the house,
I need ye rather badly,
I'll have ye squeaking like a mouse!

A highly polished table,
With highly polished chairs,
This will do quite nicely, ken
I'll no' take ye upstairs.

Lift yer skirts and let me in,
There's no one here to see,
Eight feet of wood, and it's all yours,
'Tis fine mahogany!

I will make a feast of you
I will not need a chair,
Ye'll be polishing the fine veneer,
Until yer arse is bare.

We need no bed or potting shed,
What a place tae dine!
Ye'll feel it hard under yer skirts,
Now get yerself supine!

What has happened to Lord John?

Thinking On Ones Feet

Get up! The click of rifles,
Are they aiming at my head?
Oh shit! I fear I'm captured,
One false word, I'm dead.

Rebels by their colour,
I need to form a plan,
What can I say to save myself.
I am, a wanted man!

I was captured by the British,
I was trying to enlist,
(Then some great brute with ginger hair
Beat me with his fist.)

I would join the rebel army,
Please release me from these chains,
I am for the cause of freedom,
(Just my own, if I use brains!)

Peleg Woodward seems a gentleman,
(A Reverend with a gun)
Bertram Armstrong at your service sir.
(This bargain might prove fun!)

They believe the quite unthinkable,
I must have an honest face,
(What they can see, that is not bruised,
must have the truth erased.)

John Greys alter ego,
Constructed in a trice,
An expert in the game of lies,
It won't bear inspection twice!

A coat may change its colour,
That would not be indiscreet,
I am NOT disloyal to the crown,
Just thinking on my feet!

Remembering the last time Jamie was forced to wear a uniform.......

A Coat of Red (reprise)

It burned across my shoulders,
It sent shivers down my spine,
It burned my soul and boiled my blood.
With every tailored line,

The buttons and the braiding,
Sit ill upon this breast,
I feel its lining itching.
As it rubs against my chest.

Stitches of the devil,
More lashes stung my back,
Made my flesh creep on my bones.
Made my soul turn black.

'It suits you Captain Fraser,
A fine figure of a man.
It marks you as an Officer,
All part of Tryon's plan.

He has ordered me tae wear it,
But this coat of red I shun,
As he says there is the law,
And there is what is done.

'Tis an act of subjugation,
But I cannot refuse,
Tryon, puppet master,
Pulls strings which light the fuse.

The spark of revolution,
Will kindle in the blood,
A nation crying freedom,
Amongst the bullets and the mud.

This time it was so much different!

Blue Is The Colour

Sassenach, what do ye think?
Tell me, din nae fash!
Tall and lean and handsome,
He does cut quite a dash.

There's something about a uniform
Which makes my hormones stir,
So much has happened since the last,
The memory is a blur.

The tailoring impeccable,
a perfect fit at that,
Complete with sash and waistcoat.
He's even got the hat!

I will always be a soldiers wife,
I shall follow you 'til death,
Do not try to stop me,
That would be a waste of breath!

Kiss me general Fraser,
Sear my very core,
Make your shield my love for you,
Carry it to war.

I will be there with you,
I will do what I must,
And in my dreams try not to see
Your body in the dust.

I'll stitch your wounds, I'll mend your bones
I'll try to keep you whole,
I'll even offer up a prayer,
If that will help your soul.

You will always be a soldier,
It's just what some men do,
At least this time I know we win,
And at least that coat is blue.

Washington invites himself to dinner!

Epicurean

A table laid for dinner,
Nothing but the best,
Washington has come to dine,
Along with all the rest.

Gilbert talks of pickles,
The general talk is war,
But lets us speak of what's to come,
Not what has gone before.

The voices of experience
Must be brought into play
Uniforms and manners
Will not win the day.

A flag, not just a scrap of cloth,
Stars and Stripes a call.
A hand stitched cry of freedom
A hope for one and all,

Lee would talk deployment,
Make sure his plans are sealed
With shots served up in crystal.
Before men take the field,

A toast is drunk to victory,
The leaders take their ease,
I hope there's more to Lafayette,
Than epicure and cheese!

We fought for freedom once before,
Led by idiots and fools.
All grand ideas and stratagem
Etiquette and rules.

This War will be a pickle
Its scent to some, appeals,
To others, an acquired taste
A bit like jellied eels.

General Fraser realises the burden of his latest command

Three Hundred Men

Claire I have three hundred men
Under my command,
I've orderlies and runners,
And a regimental band!

I've lieutenants and I've messengers,
I've staff who must kowtow!
And a boy tae load ma pistols,
As if I've forgotten how!

I've militia armed with axes,
Of rifles they are bare,
They're used tae catching rabbits,
Aye, one even has a snare,

They can't fight the British army,
With a pitchfork and a pole,
If I teach them how tae fight as one,
I just might keep them whole.

They've several days of drilling,
Before we take the field
I pray they learn tae take commands.
Make discipline a shield.

Now, Talking of deployment,
Claire, take me to bed
Or maybe pour another dram,
And some tasty cheese instead!

In the books Jamie and Claire take a reflective walk along the river
and talk about life...

The Void

How often will we take a breath,
And stare into the void
Look with dread over the edge,
Our sense of worth destroyed,

The point of your existence,
The reason for your life,
Your fear of death, of nothingness,
Will cut you like a knife.

How life is treated cheaply,
Wasted, thrown away,
Does no one have a duty,
To try at least to stay.

I know that he has seen the void,
More frequently than I,
A warriors end is purposeful,
He is not afraid to die.

Tears are running down my face,
I cry without a cause
Are my efforts pointless,
Healing at deaths door.

Is the night sky not a void?
He tries to draw me out
Look up and you see the stars,
They will not go out.

Nothing is ever lost ye see,
Mankind will always hope,
we exist just the same,
With all of this we'll cope.

We hear the sound of music,
The chiming of a bell,
I must check on my patient
Nine o'clock and all is well.

Life will go on around us,
We will not give up the fight,
Don't look down at the darkness,
Look up, to the light.

~

Jamie reflects before the battle of Monmouth

Remembering

I remember when my mother died,
I saw her laid to rest,
My dead wee brother with her,
Cradled on her breast,

The women made her ready,
Prepared tae meet the Lord,
Braided hair and linen shroud,
Was not what Da preferred.

I watched him as he said farewell,
And undid all they'd done,
Spread her hair about her,
Nestling their son.

Her face looked white as birch bark,
Like the pillow 'neath her head,
Her spirit was no longer there,
'Twas already with the dead.

Her hair was all about her,
The colour still sae bright,
Fiery red, Mackenzie red,
With not a streak of white.

131

Sassenach, my brown haired lass
You have yer share of grey!
Those silver streaks show you alive,
To face another day.

I will rise and lead my men,
Knowing that you wait,
Each wounded man reminding you
Of what could be my fate.

I hope folk will find nothing,
Should they care to look.
From what I've read it is the dead,
Who fill the history book.

Jamies always takes his dead into battle with him. I wrote this one from his mother's POV.

Ellen's Prayer

Well, my bonnie cockerel,
What does life hold for thee?
Red haired, smiling in yer sleep.
What dreams do ye see?

I ken ye are a special one,
One born tae be free,
Tae spread yer wings and make yer mark.
Far across the sea.

But ne'er forget the old land,
The soil where you were born,
This will always be yer home,
Though from it ye'll be torn.

Now sleep James Alexander,
My fiery second son.
The gods of old watch over you,
Your thread of life is spun.

Tall like a McKenzie,
But more Fraser like as not.
Blood and bone and all yer heart,
Declare ye are a Scot.

Walk between the fires,
Tread a path through war,
Go safely where your dreams will lead.
I cannot ask for more.

Now sleep, the sleep of angels,
Yer smile would break my heart.
Your mother's love wrapped round you,
As it has been from the start.

Yer destiny will find you,
She will be yer wife,
Sweet boy, I shall watch over you,
Where e'er you go in life.

Introducing Jane and Fanny

Sisters

I will not let them have you,
Sell you for their pleasure!
You shall not have a life like mine,
Your childhood you should treasure,

Men who would pay much in gold
To say they were your first,
Rough, sadistic, bullies,
Men seen at their worst,

I will keep you from them,
I will never yield,
I will take their punishment,
Your body I will shield.

Harkness will not find you,
We will leave this place
Your Maidenhead will not be his,
We must leave without a trace.

William will protect us,
You will not come to harm
He is a man of honour
And not a little charm.

But Harkness paid the madam,
A fatal price he'd pay
My thithter kept her promise
With what she did that day.

135

She left his body lifeless,
Butchered by the act
we fled out of the window,
My virginity intact.

Wiyum, wiyum help me,
They've taken her away,
They will hang my thithter,
At dawning of the day.

He went, he tried to save her,
She wath dead behind the door
She gave her life to save me
Fwom a lifetime ath a whore.

The man whose arms suwound me
Who maykth me feel at home,
Thith family who taykth me in
Are Wiyums folk I know

He called Lord John hith father
When we bewied Jane,
He looks like Mr Fwaser
And that to me ith plain

He pwomised to look after me,
I cannot ask for more,
I hope that when I'm older,
They won't thell me as a whore.

William has arrived back at camp to find that he has visitors

Dirty Laundry

A rumpled, unkempt Ellesmere
A sartorial offence.
A ticking off, a dressing down
For dirt and scruffiness.

Not handy with the clothes brush,
Nor the washings of a tub,
Williams laundry lies in heaps.
No laundress, there's the rub.

Fortes Fortunate Juvat.
We thought we'd take a chance.
So knew that this encampment,
Signalled the advance.

At your service Frances,
Are you not one of the whores,
In return for my protection,
You could do domestic chores.

A lifetime in a brothel,
In some ways a sheltered life,
When Harkness came for Fanny
I was waiting with a knife.

The dead no longer trouble us,
But I am on the run,
Is this knowledge safe with you,
Or is our story done

A whore does not do laundry,
A fancy whore at that,
Undresses William with a gaze,
Just like a Cheshire Cat!

Confessions of a Whore

Yes sir, I've earned wages,
I know what men should pay,
She listed acts no lady should,
I'm stumped for what to say!

As to what my wage is worth,
How am I to know?
What things cost or what to buy.
Her chagrin starts to show.

When have I done laundry,
A whore is paid to f*ck
I'll do anything your lordship likes,
Sweet Jane, you're out of luck.

My tunic needs a good brush down,
My shirts all need a scrub,
My stockings are disgusting,
My small clothes need a rub.

Then it all needs ironing,
I'm dressing to impress,
In front of Captain Richardson,
I cannot look a mess.

She handed me the basket,
All my laundry clean!
She winked an eye and curtseyed,
What she said was quite obscene.

I will not go to bed with you,
That's not part of the deal.
You are not my whore, it cannot be
Despite the way I feel.

But all men need some action
Before they go to war.
Are you then a coward sir,
I've seen it all before.

Then she told me they were leaving,
With words that fell like stone
If you can't see us to New York sir,
We shall go there on our own

I can protect a laundry maid,
I can't protect a whore.
You cannot earn your living Jane,
As you did before.

Leopards and Spots

I can tell you what the coins are sir,
And the service they will buy,
But I cannot say their value.
Tis true, I do not lie.

I grew up in the brothel sir,
My wages not my own,
Madge the madam keeps it all,
Even now I'm grown.

I know the cost of some things,
The price of all my parts,
What the shillings of the king will buy
In terms of whores and tarts!

Six of them will buy my c**t
My mouth will cost you three
And if my arse is your desire,
One pound, that has to be.

There is one thing no man can buy,
For any price in gold,
I would see that bastard dead
Before my sisters virtue sold.

Should your lordship send me shopping,
I would go, of course,
You could send me for a loaf of bread,
I might come back with a horse.

Honourable William,
Listens while she plots
This whore is like a leopard
She cannot change her spots,

New life, New York, we go alone,
Coquettishly she flirts.
Her services are best in bed,
Not washing Williams shirts.

The continental army has deployed - Rachel and Claire prepare for battle.

Women at War

Two women face a time of war,
Each with different views,
Each awaits a husband,
Each anticipates the news.

One has learned of courage
When death must show its face,
The other, sees the worst side
Of the human race.

Jamie goes past duty's call,
Inspiring his men,
He must play the hero.
And I must wait, again.

Ian, he may hesitate,
Not act when he should,
For me he forsakes violence,
He tries to act for good.

Thee would be left in desolation
A knife stuck through your soul,
How would thee cope how would thee grieve,
What would keep thee whole.

I would be left empty,
If for me he failed to act,
My conscience clear, my husband dead
My principles intact.

Rachel we can only wait,
We women play our part,
We patch them up and heal their wounds
And that is just the start.

Our men know how to fight a war,
As we do, in our way,
With sutures, and with bandages
And when all else fails, we pray!

Meanwhile Lord John appears to have joined the rebels.........and is
found in the ranks by Claire

Eye Eye

Look up to the ceiling,
Now look left and right,
You are going to need some faith in me,
If I am to save your sight!

You've a fracture in your orbit,
Your rectus muscle pinched,
That is why, you've a static eye,
You can't move it an inch.

Slimy like a hardboiled egg,
I'll need to take it in my grip.
Twist it out and ease it free,
Take care my hand won't slip.

The honey is to lubricate,
It may also stop infection,
Prepare yourself, no Laudanum
Or pain relief injection!

Jamie, hold him steady,
Make sure to hold him well,
When I dislocate his eyeball,
It is going to hurt like hell!

145

William has been duped by Richardson and taken captive – Lord John and Ian to the rescue.

Spotswood

I lie here on a floor of earth,
A sack over my head,
Wooden gag between my teeth,
But two of *them* are dead.

Taken as a hostage,
Am I Lost without a trace!
Who will Ransom William.
Who even knows this place

Who ever heard of Spotswood,
Who will find me here,
No one knows I'm missing,
This is dire straits I fear.

Voices, and in English,
With an accent, I detect.
Will these bastards sell me on,
They are deserters I suspect.

Now they ask for money,
A bargain being struck,
If this goes wrong then I am lost
And truly out of luck.

I never saw a pistol
Pulled with such aplomb,
My life is saved, the Hessians dead.
Is that really you Lord John!

A father with on a mission,
With an Indian scout for bye!
What has he been up to
Piratic patch over one eye.

That mohawk calls me cousin
They free me from my chains
Is there an explanation,
My father is at pains!

He talks of family honour,
Tis a family I should shun,
I use his name, and that is all.
Common blood, we've none.

A pawn, because of who I am,
Blackening my name.
But who am I, I am a lie
A living breathing shame!

Back at camp Lord John tries to speak with William about his father.

Truth and Reputation

I have been taught to speak the truth,
Now I see with my own eyes,
The foundations of my childhood,
Are just a pack of lies.

Ransom, Ellesmere, Fraser!
What is one more name!
I carry tack like Mac the Groom,
All I feel is shame.

I have no reputation,
Not one that I can own,
YOU are NOT my father sir,
I truly am alone.

It was all in your best interest,
You could not know the whole,
One day maybe you'll understand,
Those lies are heavy on my soul.

You truly are a Fraser,
I see it in your eyes,
In your manner, and your look,
It's him I recognise.

No finer man was ever born
Albeit he is a Scot,
He will always be a rebel
Deny that I cannot.

I am no traitor to my King
I don't fight against the Crown.
Now let me have the bottle, Dad!
Let my sorrows drown.

Life is not simple, William.
I am no judge to say.
He lived a life just to survive.
Cheat death for one more day.

He has a code of honour,
Of loyalty and truth.
I have known him many years,
Even in my youth.

The world is not in black and white,
Please William, listen, try
I raised you as a father should.
You'll be a Grey until you die.

We are not born with reputation,
It is something we must make.
James Fraser has a fine one.
Of that make no mistake,

Meanwhile Ian Murray wrestles with his conscience - and a Hessian deserter!

I Killed a Man Today

He said I would regret it,
When I gifted him his life
Now here I am hands on his throat
Reaching for a knife.

No time now for mercy,
I followed him with ease,
A cowardly, deserter,
Fleeing through the trees.

I ken I promised Rachel,
But this is a time of war,
I'll not be looking o'er my shoulder
The way I did before.

That man swore a vengeance,
He is in league with spies.
Now my hands are wet with blood,
The life has left his eyes.

To take a life will mark your soul,
I felt that mark today,
To tell my wife I broke my word,
I killed a man today!

Fanny has bad news for William...................

Protection

William! Where were you,
While you were gone, they came!
William! They took her,
William! This is not a game.

You promised us protection
You must do something PLEASE!
She is the only thing I have,
I beg you, on my knees!

A culley from the brothel,
He knew her as a whore
He said that she killed Harkness,
Said he'd seen her before!

They have taken her for murder,
This cannot wait 'til morn,
WILLIAM they will hang her,
As soon as it is dawn.

Frances, Fanny, dry your tears,
I will try my best,
Calm yourself and let me think,
This truly is a mess.

I'll ask papa, he has the rank,
He can sway these things
But to save a whore from hanging,
May be one too many strings.

Is there no one who will help me,
Who will come to Fanny's aid,
A man who lived outside the law,
To ask him, I am afraid.

Would he play the criminal,
For a bastard and a whore,
Why should he risk his freedom
He owes me nothing more.

I have no other option,
I have no other plan,
How can I let that poor sweet child,
Watch her sister hang!

Meanwhile Brianna is taking direct action back in Scotland.........

Shot In The Dark

Burglars in the bedroom,
A shotgun finds its mark
Fiona and the children,
Danger in the dark!

Go! You can'nae stay here,
Flee as best ye can,
As far away as Inverness,
In Ernie's battered van.

Best ye go tae Boston,
Is Fiona acting dumb,
She knows full well where Roger's gone,
She knows what is to come!

Rob Cameron is tenacious,
Gold fever has him strong,
'Gainst a shotgun toting Fraser,
He'll not be lasting long.

A tangled web of intrigue,
Where unseen travellers lurk,
Frenchman's gold or freedom,
Some evil is at work

Meanwhile things are starting to resolve themselves in Lallybroch in 1739 Bree makes a decision! Roger sends a letter.

Back To The Future

Meanwhile back at Lallybroch,
Roger starts to pray
Send a letter from the past,
Hope it arrives today!

Buck is in a quandary,
He ponders on his life,
Does he stay or does he go,
Is it unfair to his wife!

Bree is taking action,
Children at her side,
Find your father Mandy
It's been a rocky ride.

I won't leave Esmeralda
She'll be frightened all alone,
She's just a doll, she must stay here
She can't go through the stone.

I guess she is too modern,
With all that bright red hair,
We can't take from the future,
I know it isn't fair.

Focus on your father,
Like you did with Jem,
Hold this gemstone tightly,
We Stick together hen!

A mothers good instruction,
Falls on deafened ears,
As Mandy launches at the stone,
And promptly disappears!

Buck tells us more of his life before Alamance.............

Shotgun Wedding

I was never fair tae Morag,
Though I loved her with ma life,
She hankered fer another man,
She should ha' been his wife

I had a way wi women then,
I ken't she liked me well,
But she did na' love me,
She was in another's spell.

Drink taken at a ceilidh,
And Donald off his heid,
He got caught up wi' another lass,
And beaten 'til half deid.

And so, I found wee Morag,
The strammash was over then,
In tears behind the cow byre,
I was comfort. Do ye ken?

Well, it was more than comfort
If ye get ma drift,
We both had strong drink taken,
I was quickly in her shift.

156

Cut tae two months later,
Things that were nae in ma plan,
Her brothers had a shotgun,
I became a marrit man.

But her heart was wi' another,
I could na keep her bye,
So, I took her to the colonies,
Tae keep her from him, aye.

We never had much luck there,
And after Alamance,
we all shipped back tae Scotland,
When we had the chance.

Your family is ma' family,
Best she believes me dead,
She'll be happier wi' Donald,
So, I'll stay wi' you instead.

I can take a message,
Tell her where ye are,
Tis only a wee jump in time,
Really not that far.

But ye really should ha' told me,
When I met that murderous bitch
And my father is the war chief,
And my mother is that witch.

157

Claire sees General Fraser off to war..... but things are different

Gut Feeling

Fear and foreboding
A feeling in my gut,
Not quite really something wrong,
Just a door that's not quite shut.

I have kissed him often times
Before he's marched to war,
This time I feel empty,
I haven't felt this way before.

Creeping fear lies in me,
Gnawing at my wame,
I pray to god and all above,
He doesn't feel the same.

Twas he that saw the crossfire,
Twas me that heard the shot,
Tween the rebels and the British,
Hospital or not.

My clock had stopped, my time stood still
I felt the ooze of blood,
Staring into blaze blue eyes,
And lying in the mud.

Back at the battle of Monmouth Claire is making an impression on
Dr Leckie

Grudging Respect

He has a sucking chest wound,
Get him on the table,
Madam he has ringing ears,
He'll come round when he's able.

If you must nurse him madam
I must supervise,
Please put down that scalpel,
You'll take out someone's eyes.

Incision made, then cannula
Through the chest wall press,
A puff of air, a glob of puss
A lung relieved from stress.

Madam have you any grease,
To lubricate his burns,
Then leave them open to the air,
There are some things you could learn!

That burn will need a dressing,
We must stop infection now,
If you are unsure of procedures
I can show you how.

159

Leckie turns upon his heel
His exit lacking grace.
Doctor Fraser in full flow
Has put him in his place.

Insufferable Woman

Insufferable woman,
I order you to leave
We have orders to evacuate,
I ask you to believe!

Infuriating woman,
We are in the line of fire,
The redcoats are approaching,
We shall soon be in the mire.

Stubborn headed woman,
You can do no more
A platoon of British infantry
Is marching to our door.

I tell you Dr Leckie,
I will not leave this man,
I've a duty to my patient,
To save him if I can.

I will stay here with him,
Even if he dies,
I could not leave him to his fate,
Looking in deaths eyes.

Frustrating bloody woman!
Would you have me beg,
Please retreat behind the lines,
This place a powder keg!

I concede you are a surgeon,
A fine one, I can see,
Pick up your bag and leave that man,
I beg you, come with me.

Doctor, for you are one
Lady you are not!
I leave you in the line of fire
Take care, you don't get shot!

Hold Your Fire

HOLD YOUR FIRE!
Let them go,
thank god they're in retreat,
Sassenach, I see ye!
The wounded at yer feet.

HOLD YOUR FIRE!
Din'nae taunt them,
Let them on their way,
Sticks and stones and Redcoat scum!
We have won the day!

HOLD YOUR FIRE!
Do as I say! Am I no' in command,
This is a hospital, a church.
My wife is close at hand!

CHRIST SASSENACH!
MEN! HOLD YOUR FIRE!
The Redcoat takes his aim,
The Generals eyes locked with his wife's.
Both the eyes of pain.

A groping hand, a bullet wound.
A body racked in shock,
Surgeon can you heal yourself?
Those eyes maintain their lock.

163

He washed his hands and left her,
Said he could do no more!
May the devil eat his liver
Filthy faithless whore!

So General Lee is fuming,
Returning I am not.
Lee has not experienced
An incandescent Scot.

Sassenach I will na leave,
My hands can't stem the flood,
I have no quill and parchment,
I shall resign in blood.

So much and from one so small
To all the gods I pray,
Dinnae send yer angels yet,
They'll no' take her away.

I hear ye call for someone
Someone! Run and find the man,
If someone else than God can help,
Only Denzil Hunter can.

Flint Locked

Eyes locked across the boneyard
The whistle of the shot,
Time slows to a standstill
The earth spins to a stop.

One of us is bleeding,
I read it in your eyes
Is it me or is it you?
Is this our demise.

A hand pressed to a body,
A spreading pool of red
Sassenach, Twas meant for me!
Twas me who should be dead.

Jamie, is this dying
My body is in shock,
My surgeons brain on overtime
I'm trying to take stock.

My blood runs through my fingers,
It puddles on the floor
Jamie do not leave me now.
Death is opening her door.

I knew today was different,
Something was not right,
The void seemed ever closer,
Now I must fight gods light.

I heard the crack of gunfire,
I did not feel the ball,
I thought it would be you my love,
Answering this call.

Denny, get me Denny
Only he will do,
Denny has the skills for this,
He can get me through.

What Rachel brought from Lafayette,
Make a dressing of the cheese,
'Tis rich in penicillium
Infection it will ease.

Internal diagnosis,
Her surgeons mind is sure,
Now say a prayer, to bring her home.
to face the void once more

Gut Shot!

It hit me like a freight train,
A bolt out of the blue,
The world turned in slow motion,
My insides boiled like stew

Burning, searing, terror,
A red hot trail of dread,
Have I been shot? My hand feels blood,
My side is turning red,

I heard his cry across the field,
He must have seen me fall,
A howl of desperation,
Caused by one musket ball.

The soldier I was stitching
Left, lying on the ground.
The suture and the needle,
Left hanging from his wound.

The world is turning slowly,
In and out of focus,
Hot and cold are merged as one
Unconscious hocus pocus...........

Sassenach! No – a Dhía!
Why is she outside!
The Church is where there's safety,
She's hit! – she cannot die!

Where the hell's the surgeon,
Someone stop the blood,
Stay with me Claire, keep breathing,
Yes – in – and out – is good.

Keep the pressure on the wound,
Help her, someone, now!
I'd heal her with my own two hands,
But God, I don't know how!

General sir, your wanted!
The messenger will yell!
My wife is more important,
Tell Lee to go to hell!

I wrote my resignation
In blood upon his skin,
General Fraser is no more,
I must attend my kin.

Thank God for Denny's steady hands,
And for the power of prayer,
Laudanum and Roquefort cheese,
And the stubbornness of Claire.

She lives to see another day,
Weak and burned by fever,
My commission is resigned,
For I could never leave her!

Resignation

My wife was lying on the ground,
A lead ball in her side,
I saw her fall, I heard the shot,
I feared that she had died,

Lee's messenger was babbling,
I'm wanted on the field,
Tell General Lee to go tae hell,
On this I will na yield,

Claire is lying, ashen,
Her face a mask of pain.
I din nae care what orders come,
I'll not leave her again.

To hell with talk of cowardice,
Desertion, yes and treason.
I've been a traitor all my life,
Is my wife no a good reason.

I tell the lad take off his shirt,
I see the whiteness of his back,
My wife's blood puddled on the floor,
I can make use of that.

I write my resignation,
On skin, with blood for ink.
And send my final message back
Before I've time tae think,

I'm done with all the fighting,
General Fraser is no more,
Ye left my wife tae work outside,
In the middle of a war.

And if Lee sends another,
If it doesn't go as planned,
Tell General Lee to fetch his gun,
He'll shoot me where I stand.

Surgeons Skill

Can ye save her Denzil,
I can'nae watch her die.
She is my blood, she is my life.
Can ye at least try.

Bespectacled, determined
Instruments out,
Boiled and sharp as hers would be,
He knows his stuff, no doubt.

By the light of candles
With some help from the moon
The surgeon probed and prodded.
He would not act too soon.

A steady hand, a forceps.
He reaches for the ball
My Sassenach, she hardly breaths
I can'nae let her fall.

A small thing, insignificant,
A shot sized piece of lead
A piece of cloth, a drip of blood.
Deaths voice spins in my head.

Standing at the sideboard,
He spreads her clothing out,
The pieces fit, we have it all.
I feel the need to shout!

The ball is whole, no worries there,
No poison to inject,
Just the smell of Roquefort,
Will the atmosphere infect.

He dressed her side quite lightly
I felt his breathing ease,
Stitches and a dressing
He packed the wound with cheese.

She stirs, he lips are moving,
Sassenach are ye well.
'As you would say, 'I think I'll do,
But it hurts like bloody hell'

Penicillium Roqueforti

Pungent king of cheeses,
Some say the cheese of kings,
Fromage tres maloderant,
The French adore such things.

Made from milk of finest sheep,
Matured in southern caves
Tinged with blue, and tasty too
It's smell is for the brave!

All the training and the knowledge,
Of a surgeon with a knife,
Cannot fight infection
In the battle for a life.

This creamy French concoction,
Which smells like Parisian drains,
Is manna sent from angels,
It has healing in its veins.

Pack it in a poultice,
And with help from the gods,
Penicillium Roqueforti
Will help reduce the odds,

A patient on the table,
A surgeon makes his plan.
Like a rabbit in the headlights,
A general holds a hand.

Jamie let me do my work,
She will live another day,
But just so I am certain,
May I suggest you pray.

Pray St Luke is listening,
And while you're on your knees
Say one for General Lafayette,
For sending her that cheese!

When Ye Were Not Watching

Ye could nae see me watching,
Drawn there from afar,
Like a moth to candle flame,
To you my guiding star.

Ye could nae see me searching,
Lost in life's dark maze,
Emerging from its darkness,
I held you in my gaze.

Ye did nae ken I needed you,
As flowers need the rain,
Purgatory endless,
You could salve the pain.

Ye would nae say ye felt the same,
Yer heart as lost as mine,
My eyes met yours and locked there,
Surely fates design.

Ye will nae leave me Sassenach,
I will nae let ye go,
Our time on earth, no time at all,
For endless love tae grow,

Ye will nae be without me,
When death throws out it's lures
My body gone, bone of my bone
My soul will join with yours.

Ye did nae see the way I watched,
From that day we met,
There could nae be another then,
There has nae been one yet.

Ye do nae need tae worry,
When all of life is gone,
I'll hold you safe wrapped in my arms,
My body keeps you warm,

Do ye not remember,
The night ye made yer mark,
Wrapped in plaid in front of me,
That long ride through the dark.

I will nae live without ye,
Ye know ye keep me whole,
Two halves joined by endless love,
One mind, one life, one goal.

Ye ken I'm none sae brave as then,
We've both been through some wars,
I've not the energy of youth,
To settle up old scores,

Come lie with me, I need ye,
Our bodies will enmesh
I possess ye and I worship ye,
Oh, mistress of my flesh.

Claire is coming round...........

Unconscious Thoughts

I am just below the surface,
I hear but cannot speak,
I feel your desperation,
I am so very weak.

You talk of blood, you talk of life
Sometimes I hear you cry,
Your love is such it breaks my heart,
Perhaps to live I'll try.

I know you paid attention,
Though you may not understand,
That blood is not transfused through skin,
By the squeezing of my hand.

Sentimental soldier,
Would you talk my pain away
Brave grandstanding hero.
I could not leave you this way.

I know the pain of losing you,
Seeing life around me melt,
Do you think that I could leave you,
Knowing how that felt..

I am breaking through the darkness,
Consciousness is nigh,
Your grip may break my fingers
I have decided not to die

Another deviation by the show....... The reappearance of Master Raymond

Cloaked in Darkness

The body heals the physical,
But what then of the mind?
It searches all its corners,
Does it fear what it may find,

Restful sleep a stranger,
My dreams are running wild,
I relive scenes from ages past,
Memories of a child.

A figure cloaked in darkness,
Mysterious as a wraith,
A quiet voice, a kiss so soft,
A man who held my faith.

He said that we would meet again
He never told me when,
For what did he apologise?
Then he was gone, again.

For I am sure I saw him,
I felt his touch on mine,
Is he faith, or is he hope
Or just a hitch in time.

What then of Master Raymond
Are these thoughts a silent scream?
Or an empty cupboard in my mind,
Now filled up with a dream.

Why was master Raymond sorry............This is just my theory!

The Price of Faith

Madonna you were dying,
I magic'd death away,
My services do not come cheap,
There was a price to pay.

There was just a flicker,
A spark of life still there,
Your perfect babe so nearly formed,
With her fuzz of ginger hair,

I did not want to take her
It was not my choice,
A higher power in control
Robbed me of my voice.

Madonna I am sorry,
For I have used you ill,
No excuse will warm my soul,
Your Faith has left a chill.

He felt you should be punished,
That I should be the man,
To rob you of your firstborn,
On command of St Germaine.

The world has turned through many years
And now the fates align
Fate and Faith go hand in hand,
It is by the gods design.

Cherish then this grieving child
For her all Faith is gone,
Love her as you would your own
And help me to atone.

Kidney Function

No more water Jamie,
I think I need to pee,
Quickly fetch the bucket,
Then leave the rest to me.

Sassenach you're kitten weak
You'll fall upon yer face,
You've seen to me in much worse times,
Help is no disgrace.

Do ye need a candle
To check that all is clear,
Kidney function normal,
Now back tae bed my dear

Now ye talk of elephants,
On the point of death, they mate
I appreciate the sentiment
But ye are not thinking straight.

I will lie beside ye,
Ye'll be snug under ma arm,
Din'nae get no daft ideas,
At least I'll keep ye warm

We'll have no talk of pachyderms
Making shift to die,
If one should ever pass this way,
I'll know the reason why.

Jamie and William go on a mission..............

Last Resort.

They'd taken Jane for murder,
This was my last resort,
She'd admitted that she killed him,
There had been no Court.

There were no strings the Greys could pull,
They'd hang her in the morning,
Only one man left to ask,
To help before days dawning.

I knocked the door and waited,
Mother Claire let me inside,
He didn't hesitate to come,
He was straight by my side.

Yes, he asked some questions,
Then he made a plan,
What should I expect of him,
He's a criminal, this man.

Does he save a fellow murderer,
The dangle from the noose,
Or does he risk his all for me,
To help me spring her loose.

He certainly has all the skills
To break her out of jail,
He knows that he would hang, himself,
Should this mission fails.

Jane has died by her own hand,
In a pool of her own blood,
I could not save her from this life,
Though I believed I could.

He is sympathy and kindness,
He prays over the dead,
A lock of hair for Fanny,
He trims it from her head.

Time is short, dawn comes soon,
We cannot be caught here,
I've learned a lot about this man,
Who holds his family dear.

Is there a place for Fanny
In this family too
I will take her to the Frasers,
They will know what to do.

Welcomed in with open arms,
There are no questions asked.
Strong Scottish arms look after her.
Fanny safe at last.

Jane had no trial, but the gutter press managed to get an interview........

False Confession

Fifty two, a pack of cards,
Half Red and half black.
It takes a whore to work a trick
On the joker in the pack.

Sir you write your story,
But you won't get more from me,
Before your broadsheet is in print,
They'll hang me from a tree.

You will not tell my story,
You are the gutter press,
Anything to sell your words,
To you I won't confess.

I will have no trial,
Who will fight my case,
This is the last day I will feel,
The sunlight on my face.

I will tell you nothing sir,
Except that I am glad,
And I would do it all again,
For he was truly bad.

Would you taunt me with my sister,
What is she to you,
A lever, just to loosen lips,
To make me see this through.

You'll write your story anyways,
How I stabbed him like a ham,
Slit his throat like a butchered hog.
Go Print it and be damned

Janes last night on earth...........

Condemned

Tonight, I saw the moon and stars
Dancing in the sky,
I saw our mother one last time,
Then I drained the bottle dry.

I felt the blood run down my arms,
I felt fear drift away,
This night I have felt more alive,
Than any other day.

The dragonflies were dancing,
I saw the northern lights,
Or were they just imaginings,
Like fairy fire sprites.

Sister do not fear for me,
The good Lord knows my soul,
And any whore will tell you,
That a hole, is just a hole.

Wherever they may bury me,
With you I am not dead,
For you will keep my memory,
Inside your pretty head.

Remember all the happy times,
Dwell not on the bad,
Live your life, the best you can,
Sister don't be sad.

I will never have regrets,
I would do it all and more.
My sister Frances Pocock
Will never be a whore.

View from a prison window,
The last that I will see,
I will not be controlled by men,
They've had their piece of me.

William is still confused by his feelings for Jamie.........

Stinking Papist

Is it fate which ties us,
Our paths seem linked and crossed,
He turns up, unexpectedly,
Every time I'm lost!

Cousin, did he call me?
Now I see it's sense,
Scottish, bloody Mohawk,
His painted gaze intense.

My mind cannot make sense of this,
It whirls around my brain,
Every time I think of it
It only causes pain,

Am I a stinking papist,
Did Mac give me that name,
He and General Fraser,
Are they one and the same

Uncle Hal respects him,
Papa is his great friend,
That Scottish Mohawk is his kin,
On whom can I depend?!

He that shot my hat off,
It might have been my head,
He that spoke in Gaelic
At my Brigadiers bed.

191

Those wooden beads I threw at him,
I miss them round my neck,
In times of pain and trouble
My hand goes there to check,

To cast aside my heritage,
To put aside my life,
Accept my sire is who he is,
And she not Papa's wife.

Mother Claire, is Mother Claire,
Whichever path I choose,
And she's a constant they both love,
And one I would not loose!

The question he won't answer,
Will remain unsaid,
I'll never know exactly why,
He took mama to bed.

He calls her brave, not flighty,
Headstrong, not a whore,
He takes her blame upon himself,
A penance he'd endure,

Regretful of her passing,
Shameful of her death,
But not sorry for my birth,
I hear under his breath.

And One More Thing!

One more thing...

I beg another favour,
Before I take my leave,
You, and my mother...
And how I was conceived.

I want to know...

No decent man would tell ye,
Some things are not for sharing,
Would ye tell me your first time?
But that's not why yer caring.

I need to know....

No! I did not love her
No, it was not rape,
No, she was not married,
I'd not a cuckold make!

Did she...?

She did'nae ken the meaning,
By all the Saints above,
A headstrong girl, half my age,
She thought herself in love,

Was she....?

Did they mention she was brave?
Those who knew her well,
Courageous in her reckless way,
I heard my father tell.

Were you....?

I will do penance for her death,
Until the day I die,
Twas my fault, I am to blame
A gleam came to his eye,

Then....?

His big hard hand raised to my cheek,
He looked me in the eye,
How could I be sorry,
I am not So let it lie.

Gone...

Turned on his heel, emotion hid.
He left! his talking done.
Regretful of his actions,
But not sorry he'd a son.

Soul Searching

Searching, always searching
Something or someone,
Always some bit missing,
Incomplete, undone.

Brought up to an Earldom,
Inheriting a title,
I don't feel the joy of it,
That I'm sure is vital.

I am not my father's son,
History will recall
Not Lord John or the eight Earl
Share my blood at all,

My father is a traitor,
a Jacobite, a Scot,
Pardoned yes, but criminal
Always a rebel like as not!

Why then would I seek his help,
To free my dearest Jane
To break into a jailhouse,
See him feel my pain,

He welcomed in her sister,
No doubts, no questions asked,
His big strong arms surrounded her,
While I my feelings masked.

He says his help is always there,
If my cause is just,
I do not think he offers that,
Lightly, as he must.

Not sorry he's my father,
But sorry for his sin,
He pulls a chord inside me,
But will it draw me in.

Do I want the Earls estates,
How would I make my way,
The lawyers will look after them,
Sort out the day to day.

I've a cousin who's a Mohawk,
But he was born a Scot,
And he has married Rachel,
Fix that – I cannot.

They have a different moral code,
Which runs deep in their soul,
An honesty, a truthfulness,
Should I make that my goal.

Thoughts are whirling in my brain,
I need to sit and think,
Time to set a course in life,
Not teeter on the brink.

I left Frances with the Frasers,
When I rode off that day,
I could so easily have left her,
To live with Lord John Grey.

To see her safe and cared for,
Again, I damn that man,
Will I ever call him father
That cannot be a plan.

But for now, I'll wait and think,
And search for Cousin Ben,
My bones tell me he is not dead,
Or I'm a Scotsman ken.

Reunited

Focus on our future,
Where we need to go
Think of where your father is
Hold tight and don't let go.

Hold tight to Esmeralda
Try not to drop that jewel
Don't get lost, don't lose your grip
Separation would be cruel.

Mummy I can hear him,
Mummy over here
Daddys on the other side
I can feel him near.

I'm sure I know this graveyard,
This is Lallybroch,
This is the where, but what's the when.
Which time did we unlock.

Daddy is that really you
Is that Uncle Buck
Mandy is behind me
And Ma too with some luck.

I really miss my parents
I'd be with them again
It's not important where we live
With us it is the when

Ghosts of The Past

It is 1739 and Brian Dhu meets a ghost in the graveyard.

I can't say I'm alone here,
I've Jenny and the boy,
And lying in the hillside
The source of all my joy.

Taken from me early
At the prime of life,
My red-haired tall Mackenzie bride.
My soulmate and my wife.

The boy away to study,
He's special, that I ken,
He'll do great things when he is grown.
If he stays alive 'til then.

And Jenny - she's all Fraser
A dark one like her da.
She'll no suffer all fools gladly
That way she's like her ma.

That's done with the living,
I must attend the dead,
I Tend their final resting place
The stones that mark their bed.

Ach - Mo gradh, I see you
Moving down the path
Red hair flying as you run.
Yes I can hear you laugh!

Is that young Willie with ye?
I can see him too.
Have I died and joined ye,
Is wee Robert there with you?

My legs are weak, I'm falling
Are you real or but a ghost?
Am I lying in the heather
With the ones I miss the most..

The Unlocked Door

Grief is like an unlocked door,
Into a darkened room
A cold dark deep endless abyss,
Like life inside a tomb.

Some folk learn to lock the door,
They throw away the key,
Their sorrow kept imprisoned
That would' na do fer me.

My lost ones are still with me,
I see them all around,
In the whisper in the wind,
Their voices may be found.

I see them in the faces
Of folk who pass my way.
I ken they are not part of me,
But the thought brightens my day.

There is something about you,
Something I cannot place,
Tis not your eyes or yet your smile
Or the hair which frames your face.

It's something quite ethereal,
That only I can see,
It's just a way of being,
The way my Ellen was to me.

Is it just coincidence
I am Brian, you are Bree,
Or am I just a heart sore widower
who let his grief go free.

In the show – Brianna has a chat with Brian Fraser who notices the family resemblance.........

Family Resemblance

Are ye sure it's just by marriage,
Ye look just like ma wife,
Not just yer eyes, tis all of you,
I'd swear it on ma life.

I guess that you must miss her,
I can see I'm like you all,
I see it in her portrait
Hanging in the hall.

We thank you for your welcome,
This is a truly special place,
But I'm Mackenzie just by marriage,
The lie shows on my face.

He hugged me as a father would,
It was truly time to go,
The truth would surely kill him,
Best he does not know.

I'm Brian, she's Brianna
I watch and let it pass,
But there it is, it's in that walk,
The swaying of that arse.

204

The Frasers are not stupid men,
I am blessed with a brain,
That family has been here before,
They will come here again.

Give welcome to a stranger,
And an angel you might find,
With a husband and a family
And a very firm behind.

In the quiet of the graveyard,
There is peace amongst the stone,
While there are folk in Lallybroch,
I shall never feel alone.

Rachel and Ian decide to return to the ridge with the Frasers
and Rollo makes an exit......

Wolf Brother

Seeking out adventure,
Was like falling off a log,
For teenage Ian Murray,
And me, his faithful dog,

Lying at his bedside,
One last watch I'll keep,
Tired, worn out dreaming,
My life replays in sleep.

Wolfs Brother as a Mohawk
I've been right there by his side,
The day he laid down his old life,
And took a Mohawk Bride.

Coming home, I walked with him,
A long and sorrowed trail,
Kept him warm through lonely nights,
My loyalty won't fail.

Indian Scout – I was his right,
Protecting, by his side.
When he is lost, I'm always there,
His best friend and his guide.

I've seen the boy become a man,
We've travelled many miles,
I've protected all his family,
I've seen the children smile.

He's married now and happy,
Friend Rachel keeps his heart,
I am old and stiff with wounds,
But from him I'll not part,

My life was an adventure,
My dreams now melt like the ice,
a good life, for a half wolf dog,
A Scots boy won at dice.

I have no strength to raise my head,
I cannot thump my tail,
My time has come to join the wolves,
On the never-ending trail.

Goodbye my boy, you are a man,
Your life should make you proud,
I am still sitting on your right,
Silent in the crowd.

Jamie knows how a it feels to lose a loved one as a child.......here
he reaches out to Fanny

A Lock of Hair

I know just what she's feeling,
That awful sense of grief
The sadness and the emptiness,
For which there's no relief.

For I have seen my share of it,
Known the touch of death
I saw my mother in her grave.
Felt her final breath.

Small things for a grieving child,
A proper place to stay,
A lock of hair, a friendly face
To help her through the day.

The strength that comes from family,
Of somewhere to belong,
Somewhere to cry not hiding tears
When it's too hard to be strong.

There is a home on Frasers Ridge
A life devoid of fear,
I swear no man will harm you,
As long as I am near.

Claire hers music from the future..............which reminds her of the past.

Tiddly Om Pom Pom

A silly little ditty,
A song not from this time,
An echo from the future,
Some words of childish rhyme.

Singing in a piping voice,
I heard you loud and clear,
Only I would recognise,
That tune upon my ear.

For I liked to be beside the seaside,
I used to hum that song to Bree.
I liked to stroll all along the prom,
I loved to walk beside the sea.

In memory I've another child,
I kissed her still born head,
I sang to her those self-same words,
Had faith she was not dead.

Oh, Fanny just who are you,
That song my heart would break,
Is my Faith inside your locket,
Was her death just a mistake.

Now I hear a brass band playing,
In a bandstand in a park,
I see a gravestone by a wall
And our baby, in the dark.

Why would he be sorry,
What thing did he regret,
What did Raymond fail to tell me?
Did he think I would forget!

Book not Show
Unfortunately, a TV adaptation is not able to include everything!
Here are few things they missed.

Andy Bell the Edinburgh printer who has custody of Jamies printing
press......He's a spectacle indeed.

A Bonnie Concubine

He does nae rise 'til lunchtime,
He parties until dawn,
Wee Andy Bell will sleep away
The hours of the morn.

A man who uses ladders
To climb down from his horse,
The horse is either very tall,
Or the man is short of course!

Arrival with a flourish,
And ceremony due,
Andy Bell, come join us man,
Come and take a pew!

As short as tall men sitting down,
A conformation mess,
A twisted spine and big hooked nose,
But fashionable dress.

A formidable character,
Well-known in the town,
He jokes of his appearance,
Barely wears a frown.

Etcher and engraver,
He's not getting a pass,
This man has taken liberties
With Jamie's Bonnie lass.

He tries to pay with whisky,
And tales of Bon Viveur
There's only one thing Jamie wants,
Money is the cure.

Twelve years rent was needless
He used her from the start,
Andy Bell will pay his due,
For the Bonnie printed art.

Pressing Business

Let's get down tae business
Let's cut tae the chase,
Twill tak much more than whisky
Put a smile upon my face,

Andy Bell looked sheepish,
Ye'll have called at the shop?
Well, her work has so much beauty man
It seemed a shame tae stop.

Has ma Bonnie been yer concubine
Fer all of twelve long years,
And I've been paying lodge fer her,
Yer driving me tae tears.

I've used but no' abused her,
Ye'll find her good as new,
I'm sure there's common ground here,
The deal is there tae do.

Cut to the hotel cellar,
A stench to raise the dead,
General Frasers rotting corpse
Is leaking through the lead

Wee Andy helped me sort it,
With maggots and with bran,
The bones will get to Balnain,
With all the speed we can.

A deal was done for printing,
I mean to write a book,
I've negotiated copies
But I knew you'd want a look.

Cheeky little skinflint,
Ye'll have it leather bound,
And copies for the colonies,
A compromise was found.

Also in the package,
Himself would get to pen,
Stories writ by Grand Da,
On for the weans ken!

I scratched my head and dipped my quill
Just where would I start,
A French fop downstairs for ye ma'am
Disturbs the writer's art!

Why would Percy Beauchamp
Come calling at my door,
No good can come for Fergus
From what he knows, I'm sure.

Politics and intrigue,
Quite beyond the pale,
With Fergus in the middle,
And a country up for sale.

The Perfect Woman

She understands my every word,
Is silent unless told,
Only speaks when spoken to,
And then in typeface bold,

A lady with a subtle tongue,
In language she's adept,
Guided by her masters hand,
Around the law she stepped,

A body formed of iron cast,
A heart of hardened steel
A soul baptised in font of lead,
Free, she will nae kneel.

I'd sheath my dirk, lay down my gun
And take her by the hand,
This canny lass will speak my mind
And broadcast to the land.

I will take her 'cross the sea,
Fair maid who does my will,
Mightier than any sword
To those who'd read their fill,

My Bonnie lass, we'll have some fun
Speak what every man desires
Spread the words of freedom,
Dance between life's fires.

When I was lost she was ma voice,
Her words would tell my life,
Obedient in every way,
Much more so than ma wife,

The Other Woman

My master loves me dearly,
Looks after me with care,
Keeps me in the prime of life,
Makes sure my parts don't wear!

A beauty, made of iron
Crafted to impress,
Smooth of operation,
My workings he'll caress.

I am well versed in Latin,
Hymn sheets and the Bible
Treason written down in words
Sedition, sometimes Libel.

He rescued me from burning,
Stored by Mr Bell,
Put to use by this wee man,
At least he kept me well.

And now I travel 'cross the sea,
Satire in words to spread,
Fergus and L'onignon
I will work for them instead!

He knows my inner workings,
We fit like hand and glove
I am his other woman,
His Bonnie other love!

Fergus and Marsali and their family were also omitted from season 7 part 2...........

Quad Erat Demonstrandum

Necessity the old wives say
Is mother of invention,
How adept we have become
At hiding our intention.

All our wealth is melted down,
Mundane things are made,
Rifle shot made out of gold,
Tools of the soldiers trade.

Two sets of typeset letters,
Rolled in dirt and grease,
We would not need to do these things
If these were times of peace.

All lost in that fire,
Which someone set by stealth
A child lost, a soul that's mourned
Is worth far more than wealth

Counting up our losses,
We formulate a plan,
To get us all to safety,
Savannah if we can.

Found amongst the ruins,
A grimy bag of lead,
What use now without a press.
The printing business dead.

Caslon English Roman,
For printing things in Latin,
The font for Papist prayer books,
Which bag shall we pack that in.

He smiles and tips the letters out,
He scratches off the dirt,
A gleam of gold beneath the grime,
His face becomes alert.

Fortunes change in instants,
Poverty removed.
Quad Erat Demonstrandum
Our plan is now approved.

Another scene which didn't make the TV series!! What no Hal!!

Asthma Attack

Headquarters of the British,
I go to tell my tale,
Lord John? – I don't know where he is
I've searched without avail.

Recalled to the army,
Commission all renewed
Panic starts to grow inside,
It will not be subdued.

A man stands in the corner,
A cloud of golden lace,
Lord Johns stamp but older,
This must be 'His Grace'

Yes, my name is Harold
And yes I am a Duke,
Pardloe is the title,
My god I think I'll puke.

Welcome to the family,
With charm, my words he parried,
My dear, you must call me Hal,
I'd no idea he'd married.

Yes, he'd called on Henry,
Of course, that is his son!
And Dottie too and William,
The family visits done.

He is not here for pleasure,
His army lines the shore,
The Duke seeks out his officers
He's here to fight a war.

Pray now, where's my brother,
He asks me, nice as pie,
Believe I see straight through your face,
I will know it if you lie!

Escorted home, the truth may out,
Hal will have to wait,
Lord John is gone I know not where,
In Jamie's hands his fate.

Germaine to the rescue
The rabble are dispersed,
No one shall harm his Grannie,
For they will come off worst

The hand of fate, or providence
The Duke is robbed of breath
Asthma, a severe attack
It could lead to his death.

Breathe in two three, And out to three
Breathe long without objection,
Just concentrate on breathing
You are under my protection

Confined to bed and in my care,
This solution is quite neat,
Hal is now our prisoner
In the house on Chestnut street.

Held Hostage

I'm searching for my brother John,
He's missing, who knows where,
My blood is up, I'm fuming!
Is he kidnapped? But who'd dare!

My chest feels tight, I cannot breathe,
My remedy not working.
If I collapse out in the street,
I'll be robbed for certain.

Who is this bloody woman,
She's taken all my clothes,
She's feeding me the strangest tea
And smoke blown up my nose!

And I am in my brother's house,
At least that's what she said,
But even though I'm breathing,
She won't let me out of bed.

What's this, they're writing letters,
Pretending to be John.
I think I'm being kept here
for a reason. Hell, Anon.

This woman is my brother's wife,
How could this come to be!
Women do not serve his needs,
His queer proclivities!

Good God I've been here ages,
Sitting in my shirt,
I can hear the drums approaching,
The rebel army dirt!

These women must have necks of brass,
They're lying to the army,
Kidnapping a Lord Melton
They really both are barmy.

Lord Melton! Jenny points the gun,
Twas you that killed my man,
Locked him in a prison,
Where his lingering death began!

Softly footed as a cat,
He walked into the room,
To see his sister blazing mad,
And the Lord to meet his doom.

Without a sound, the pistol grabbed
The point blank shot diverted,
His sister Jenny thus disarmed,
A crisis is averted.

Your servant Mr Fraser Sir,
Most obedient – your grace,
I see ye've met my sister,
By the look upon yer face!

We meet Dottie......................

Force of Nature

Determined blood runs in her veins,
She will not be deflected,
No! not in her repertoire,
She will not be rejected.

English aristocracy,
Unstoppable a force,
But always very ladylike,
And genteel of course.

Her hat set at a surgeon,
An army man for sure,
But a fighting Quaker,
On the wrong side of the war.

She packs her things and follows,
Dresses in a trunk,
But plain and now plain speaking,
Does thee think her drunk!

Sweeping Denzell off his feet,
The Surgeon wears a frown,
She would travel with the army,
In a war against the Crown.

So, Lord Melton's daughter,
Travels to the fray,
Unleashed force of nature,
A Quaker – did you say!

Talking now of thee and thou,
To be a surgeons wife,
Could drive her father to his grave
Shortening his life.

Wrapped round her little finger,
He may just have to pray,
For help to tame the whirlwind
That is Dorothea Grey.

Sylvia Hardmans cabin....and Jamies bad back

Mustard Plastered

If the devil could have cast his net,
He would have caught a shoal,
Full house of rebel officers
Who only had one goal,

Enticed by Daniel Morgan
A meeting of the great,
Re-enlistment as a General
Was to be my fate.

I was bound for Philadelphia
To find my wife, of course.
Til that cheeky bastard Washington,
Commandeered my horse.

Several hours later
I'm making shift to go,
A fiery pain shot up my back
Ifrinn - it's my lumbago.

I've never had a poultice
Applied with so much heat,
Mustard and fresh horseradish,
A dhia it burns a treat.

I'm Face down on the children's bed,
Friend Hardman rubbed it in,
I'm sure I felt it's searing heat
Burning through my skin.

Two nights it took to loosen up,
I'd not live them again
Limping to the privy,
Half crippled by the pain.

Her daughters walked me to the road,
And saw me safe away,
In a load of cabbages
What a way to spend a day.

I stink of sweat, I smell of veg
And a mustard plaster dressing.
And she has gone collecting herbs
Does she try and keep me guessing.

when I find my errant wife,
I will na take excuses,
She may well find the potting shed,
Has one or two good uses.

In the books the Ian and Rachels wedding was also the wedding of Dottie and Denzil and was much more colourful.

Meeting as Friends

Uniforms and Highland dress,
Meet this time as friends,
Two families, both torn by war,
Hostilities suspend.

Two couples joined together,
In love as clear as glass,
The physician and the Duchess,
The Mohawk and his lass,

We walked along the river,
Talked as couples do,
The lassies will be sore, the morn!
Well, the men may be that too!

Denny, is a surgeon,
ye ken he'll have a book,
When Dottie asked me for advice,
I told her where to look,

What did ye tell her Sassenach,
I ken ye have yer whiles!
Ye did'nae tell her that one!
Well, that should mak him smile

And Rachel too, ye told her that
Won't Ian think it odd,
His Quaker lass, his virgin bride,
Will make him call for God,

We fell to reminiscing,
Our highland wedding night,
Not a monk he'd told me,
He didn't ken I'd bite!

He talked of natural talent,
Things I'd taught him well,
Of waking bruised and sated,
And still under my spell,

Let's go home then Sassenach,
His tongue ran up my neck,
He lit the flame inside me,
One not to keep in check,

Make me call his name out loud,
And I'll see what I can do,
I've a few tricks still up ma kilt
Tae get a squeak from you.

Ye make me say 'oh god' each day,
With things ye've done or said,
Most of them tae do with life,
And nought tae do wi' bed.

The print shop fire and Henri Christian.........

Fire

Airless night, too hot to sleep
They'd climbed into the night,
Lying back amongst the stars,
In the moonlight, bright.

Two lads, always hand in hand
Together on the roof
Brothers, siblings bound by blood
If you ever wanted proof.

Different from the others,
Loved in equal measure,
Little Henri Christian,
A child the family treasure.

A happy, carefree laughing, boy
To entertain, his goal.
Cherished and defended,
A families heart and soul

Smoke and flames, rage through the shop
Get the family out,
No one saw where they had gone,
Their future is in doubt.

But there they were stuck on the roof,
Above the loading bay,
He froze with fear, framed in the fire,
We felt the people pray.

231

He wrapped his stunted arms and legs,
Around his brothers frame,
Tried to grip, to hold on tight.
But strength was not his game.

The gathered crowd stretched out their arms,
As they saw him fall,
But none could catch the braw wee man
He fell straight through them all.

Sickening crash upon the ground,
A life gone in a stroke,
A young soul lost amongst the dreams,
And the print shop, up in smoke.

Why does he seem to take the good,
The Lord must have a plan,
There was no child that brought us joy,
Like Henri Christian

Tragedy

Smoke
I dreamed of cigarettes and Frank,
Our loft was filled with smoke,
Fire! I screamed in terror,
My sleeping man awoke!

Flames
Get out now, he yelled at me,
Don't bother to dress,
Wake the others quickly,
Get them from this mess.

Panic!
Falling down the ladder,
Landing in a heap,
Shouting, raising the alarm!
Waking all from sleep.

Fire
Fire is in the print shop,
Stacks of bibles burn,
Get the kids out Marsali,
Or we'll all cook to a turn.

Woken
Felicite and Joanie
Stir their sleepy heads,
Where are Henri and Germaine?
They haven't used their beds.

Lost
Standing half dressed in the street,
Watching our lives burn,
Where the hell are those two boys
Will they never learn.

Trapped
Emerging on the rooftop,
Trapped there by the flames
Sleeping in the starlight,
Not the best of games.

Danger
Throw your little brother!
But Henri would not go,
Terrified he looked at us
In the street below.

No!
Germaine he is too heavy,
He cannot hold on,
His little arms and shortened legs,
He really isn't strong.

Falling
He slipped so slowly from his grip,
Somersaulted down,
Fell through all the waiting arms,
Landing on his crown.

Dead
The sickening thud upon the ground,
The screaming of his mother,
The family had lost a son
Germaine, his little brother.

Arson
How was the fire started,
Was it set, to start
Fergus never left the forge
Alight when it was dark.

Rebuilding
All we have is Clarence
And what's rescued from the blaze
The clothes that we stand up in.
At least it burned my stays!

Loss.
A family in mourning,
Focussed on our thought,
The loss of Henri- Christian,
And all the joy he brought.

Leaving
We will leave Philadelphia,
Jamie take me now
back to our home Frasers Ridge,
We will find a way somehow!

Meanwhile Claire is still practicing as a doctor.

Sophronia

Brought here by her mistress,
A woman in despair,
Taken to her masters bed,
Damaged beyond repair.

Her baby cut inside her,
Her insides torn apart,
I could mend the physical,
I cannot mend her heart!

He wept, She told me he was sad,
The master of her life,
Her child lost had made him cry,
Not so, his callous wife.

Ether, Breath it deeply child,
You shall not feel the pain,
My sutures will seal up the wounds,
Make you whole again.

All sewn up, fistulae gone,
All connected right,
Should I take one extra step,
Prevent another mite.

It is her life, you saw her grief
Do not play god today
Thee can't decide her future
Don't take her choice away,

Rachel speaks compassion,
It's not my call to make,
Even when the outcome
Is another man's mistake.

Her master will still take her,
Tis not ours to decide,
She is his slave, his property,
He will not be denied

Desperation on her voice
Muffled by her hand,
I tried my best, twas not my fault
It wasn't what god planned.

Richardson is still at large......

I Spy

Blended in the background,
The ever present ear,
The eye that sees into a life,
And casts a shaft of fear,

Hiding in the shadows,
Seeking out their prey,
Every army has its spies,
Faceless men in grey,

You would not give them notice,
Standing in a room,
Chameleons of intrigue,
Blending with the gloom,

Plausible and eloquent,
Hiding in plain sight,
What colour then his coat today,
What side of the fight.

Richardson the grey man,
Has changed from Red to Blue,
From loyalist to rebel,
But is this really true.

Keep yer wits about ye,
Yer wee knife at yer side,
Already he's played games wi' you,
Made you Lord Johns bride.

238

Sassenach he'll come again,
He'll try and play ye false
God knows what and God knows how,
Din'nae join his waltz.

He found me in my surgery,
Devious, shifty man,
Cards upon the table time,
The spy outlined his plan.

He sought me as an agent,
But Jamie spoiled his game,
No longer family to Hal,
He'd use me just the same.

Pardloe lobbies London
Seeking terms for peace,
Richardson is all for war,
The fight then must not cease,

He seeks a source of blackmail
A tool to stop the Duke,
Would I give him Lord John Grey,
The thought near made me puke.

Leave this place and leave it now,
I've a patient to attend,
You will not get your dirt from me,
I don't mean to offend!

Ezekiel Richardson,
Hastened from my door
Time and tide determine
If our paths should cross once more.

The return of the British and Jamies refusal to take up arms.........

Invasion

Jamie climbed into our bed,
Just before the dawn
He smelled of marsh and fish and frogs,
And just a bit of prawn.

Good fishing then? Aye, not too bad
He told me what they saw,
Soldiers marching, troop on troop,
Warships off the shore!

The British Army landing,
A dozen men- o-war,
Here comes the revolution!
Knocking on our door.

At supper time we had a knock
The Continentals calling,
You are needed General Fraser Sir,
Their manner was appalling.

They cannot see discretion,
That their cause is lost,
Live to fight another day,
Or you will count the cost,

He will not fight, not this time,
For this is not his battle,
He sees the Continentals,
Will be rounded up like cattle.

Now accused of cowardice
The Scot is losing patience,
Dia eadarainn's an t-olc,"
Is lost in the translation.

Go with God but leave my house!
I will nae shake yer hand.
My commission is resigned,
I've told ye where I stand.

Prepare for occupation,
Not quite what we planned,
We must live with the British,
I shall keep my knife at hand.

A Frasers Ridge Christmas

This end section has no roots in either book or series.
These poems were written as a little light
entertainment for the festive season.

Christmas Cleaning

Jamie, please go hunting,
You are right under my feet,
Go and shoot some rabbits,
We could use some Christmas meat.

There's fires to lay, A tree to trim,
Rooms and beds to air,
A trunk arrived, I need some help
To get it up the stair.

Sassenach don't panic,
We always get things done,
I love tae watch ye in a flap,
Please don't spoil ma' fun.

I shall sit here in ma study,
And watch yer feathers fly
Feet up with a nice wee dram,
I can watch the world go by.

Now Sassenach be careful,
What are ye doing with that broom,
Click yer heels and stamp yer feet
Ye'll be flying round the room.

Yer hair is white as falling snow,
And tis fighting with yer head,
Ye look just like a thistle,
Or ye just got out of bed!

Now calm yerself and bide a while,
We've days tae do the work,
And for heaven's sake be careful,
What yer doing with ma' dirk.

I shall help ye in a moment,
Or I ken ye'll have ma balls,
Ye'd hang them on the Christmas tree,
Or nail them to the walls.

No, I don't need dusting,
My ears are free from grime
But some polish and a good rub up,
What a way tae pass the time!

Mince Pie Anyone?

Claire, yer looking kind o'frazzled,
There's flour in yer hair,
Or is it just completely white,
Do I need tae beware!

There's a flavour tae yer pastry,
I am no' tellin' lies,
Have ye added something medical,
Or that spray that kills the flies.

Oh! They'd just come out the oven.
Did they need tae cool,
Would temperature improve the taste,
Claire don't think me a fool!

Sassenach don't fash yersel'
We're hardly like tae die,
There's so much food we will na' starve
Fer lack of a mince pie.

Did ye rub the flour with the fat,
Mix it to a dough,
Cool it on the window ledge,
In a bowl of snow.

Did ye soak the currants well
In brandy from the keg,
Or the foul smelling liniment,
You use tae rub ma leg.

I tried tae find a proper cook,
Tae help ye for the day,
But Lord John values Mrs Figg,
He'd no' let her away!

He feared for her safety,
If he sent her tae the ridge,
That she might meet a chilly end,
Locked in Brianna's fridge!

A Magical Night

My shawl around my shoulder,
I stood out on the porch,
The night lit by a million stars,
No need for a torch.

The moon a silver sliver,
Hanging from a stardust chain,
No wind to stir the tall blue pines,
White snow lay without stain.

In the quiet of a winter night
I stared up at the sky
Crossed my fingers, closed my eyes
I let my wishes fly.

He said he'd something special,
There would be something in the air,
Listen and you'll hear it.
Make sure that you are there.

A distant jingle, harness bells,
A growing speck of light,
A flying sleigh hove into view
Its paint and harness bright.

There was something strange about it,
As it swept low oe'er the snow,
The driver dressed in tartan,
Gave a Scottish Ho Ho Ho.

The reindeers horns looked razor sharp,
And much to my surprise
They had Shaggy auburn fringes
Hanging in their eyes.

Stand well back Claire, give them room
Careful where you stand,
They have' na got their headlights on,
They can'nae see tae land.

In a vapour trail of whisky.
But With not a misplaced hoof
Gentle as a setting dove
They landed on the roof.

They're twice as swift as reindeer,
And I've eight instead of nine
With a little bit o'training
Highland Coos fly fine.

Danger! Sassenach at work.

Weans run from everywhere,
Breanna hides a smirk,
There is a sign hung on the door!
'Danger, Sassenach at work'

All the family gathered,
Hungry for a feast,
The cook is clanging pots and pans,
Like a fiend released.

Dinnae fash now Sassenach,
I'm sure all will be fine,
Just be tender with the turkey,
And go easy on the wine.

Ye've plucked it clean of feathers,
Ye've roasted it for hours,
My nose detects a smell of herbs,
That stuffing smells of flowers.

What are ye doin Sassenach,
Please put down the knife,
Tis best I carve this valiant bird,
That sacrificed its life.

Best we leave her to her work,
We should not break the spell,
Lest the smell of sulphur,
Bless a dinner born in hell!

Wondrous faces round the table,
All anticipate,
the wonderous creation,
Which is yet to grace a plate.

Get out of my kitchen!
Echoes round the halls
Best I heed the warning,
Then I might retain my balls!

Cooking Under Pressure

Dinner was a triumph,
It went without a hitch,
The turkey succulence itself,
Not bad from a witch!

Aromatic stuffing,
With chestnuts and with herbs,
A smell so damned enticing
Himself ran out of verbs.

Root vegetables all roasted,
Boiled kale in butter tossed,
All cooked to perfection
I kept my fingers crossed.

They all tucked in with relish,
Ample recompense
For every Scottish joke he'd made
At the cook's expense.

Plates were polished empty,
Gravy mopped with bread,
Lord Johns port was passed around,
Success went to my head!

I quite forgot the pudding,
Steaming in its pan,
I should have opened up the valve,
It was all part of the plan.

It shook the house foundations,
I think it woke the dead!
Brianna's new invention,
'It was quite safe' she said.

Brianna where's yer common sense,
I ken it comes in snatches,
At least ye have nae burned the house,
Thank God I banned yer matches.

Never trust a white-haired witch,
For whom cooking's not a pleasure,
To steam a Christmas pudding
In a kettle under pressure!

Have a wee dram Sassenach,
Just tae calm ye down,
I'll clean the ceiling later,
Now go and change yer gown,

While yer upstairs changing,
Could ye check the roof fer leeks,
And when ye've got a moment,
I need a change o' breeks.

There's Christmas pudding everywhere,
The walls and floor are sodden,
I've not heard a bang like that,
Since the cannon at Culloden

Situation Vacant

Din'nae fash now Sassenach,
Come and sit wi' me.
Pour yerself a glass o' port,
Sit upon ma knee.

Never mind the pudding,
If I fancy something sweet,
As long as there is honey,
And bread, we have a treat.

That was a fine spread Sassenach,
But ye've overstretched yerself,
Ye've been a roasting and a boiling.
Like some demented elf!

Yer place is at the table,
Presiding here with grace,
Not slaving at the fireside,
Sweat running down yer face.

I ken ye want tae do yer bit,
And I ken ye read a book,
But there's more than that tae catering,
Next year we hire a cook.

I think we can afford it,
It will nae cause much pain.
Tis more sensible tae pay someone.
Than tae build the house again.

Fireside Thoughts

All the bairns are off tae bed,
We linger by the fire,
Poking dreams back into life,
Watch the flames leap higher,

We share the warmth between us,
Contented in the heat,
A conversation without words,
Our lives for now complete.

Her head upon my shoulder rests,
I feel her sigh with love,
Hair a shade of drifted snow,
Whiter than a dove.

In these silent moments,
When all our thoughts are deep
Our souls align and find the stars,
Denying us our sleep.

I ken her flesh is willing,
Her face betrays her game,
She makes me think unholy thoughts,
Her eyes dance in the flame.

Come then do yer worst with me,
Until the fire dies,
Lie with me 'til the brave new dawn.
Lights the winter skies.

Sassenach you are my life,
You and you alone,
Hold my key to purgatory,
And for my sins atone.

Man does not live two hundred years,
Yet you have spanned that time.
I don't regret a single day,
Since I called you mine.

Our bones may rest beneath the earth,
But time will not erase,
The memory of the years we had,
Or the smile that lights your face.

May peace prevail in what is left,
May God answer all our prayers,
And with his mercy and with yours,
I may just get up the stairs.

Window of Opportunity

Imprisoned in the speak a word,
Boots up, in his chair,
A red-haired man, lifts a glass,
To toast a woman rare,

So ye stayed with me Sassenach,
Ye did nae join the dance,
Are we too old tae ceilidh
Do ye feel the years advance?

Here's to peace and quiet,
To whisky in the glass,
To thinking of my hands upon,
Yer lovely, rounded arse!

I ken how drinking takes ye!
Yer inhibitions fade,
Another dram, yer drawers will drop,
So din'nae be afraid!

Pull off ma boots now Sassenach,
Come make this night complete,
Did ye bring the turtle soup,
It makes ye indiscreet.

One more sip, ye'll lose yer shift,
Shall I unlace yer stays,
Run my hands down o'er yer skin,
My lips yer sweet breasts graze!

I love it when you wear the kilt,
It suits you to a tee,
Worn like a proper highlander,
Forever wild and free.

When discussing underwear,
Your plan is full of flaws,
Fair is fair, I'm wearing none!
And you aren't wearing yours!

The house is nicely empty,
This room is nicely warm,
I'll take this opportunity,
And explore your naked form!

Sassenach bend o'er the desk,
Before ye say much more,
Don't fret about intruders,
Bree already locked the door!

After The Dishes

Nothing left but washing up,
You can wash, I'll dry.
The kids are playing in the snow,
I'm weary, I won't lie.

'Tis time tae light the fire,
To pour a dram or three,
Put our feet up somewhere warm,
Oh! Did ye check under the tree.

You know I need no presents,
No expensive jewel,
I'm happy that we live in peace
To share another Yule.

To spend our life together,
Through war and peace and time,
Knowing that you love me,
Is contentment such a crime.

The greatest gift that I could have,
Is standing by my side,
Who would have thought it when we wed,
My fierce reluctant bride.

We have walked between the fires,
Made love under the stars
I can map the years in stitches,
Trace my life in your scars,

Now come and sit beside me,
Let me pour a glass,
Let's drink a toast to family,
And the year about to pass.

Take yer shoes off Sassenach,
Yer tired, ye look quite beat,
Shed yer stockings, and yer stays,
Now let me rub yer feet!

What are ye after Sassenach,
Quit wiggling yer toes,
Yer hooves smell like the farmyard,
I'd better hold ma' nose.

Is the rest of you more fragrant,
I think I'd like tae check,
What are the scents I'm like to find
If I work down from yer neck!

What is it with whisky
It makes him such a flirt!
It's hard to argue with a man
Whose head is up yer skirt!

Do Not Disturb!

We lay entangled on the hearth,
Her body wrapped in mine,
Her skin still glows like moonlight!
Ageing like fine wine.

Discarded clothing all around,
On it, firelight plays,
Boots and belts, a sporran
And an ancient set of stays.

I feel him stretch beside me,
Scars and old bones creak,
If I had to count them all,
I'd be here for a week!

Jamie it's past midnight,
In fact, it's nearly dawn,
That's not the moonlight it's the sun,
That lights a new year morn.

The sound of merry footsteps,
A tapping at the door,
Childish giggles fill the air,
We scrabble on the floor!

Happy New Year Grand Da!
Are you and Grannie on the wine!
We've been to everybody's home!
The ridge is doing fine!

I hear Roger coughing,
Clearing his throat,
One chorus then, what shall we sing?
While I hang up ma coat!

Yer Granda can'nae be disturbed,
It says so on the sign,
He's renewing an acquaintance,
For the sake of Auld lang syne.

He moves fast for an Auld one,
In his kilt he's quickly clad,
He's had fifty years of practice.
In wrestling that plaid!

My hair is quite dishevelled,
In fact, it's quite a mess,
There wasn't time for primping,
As I climbed into my dress.

Two chairs at the fireside,
Two glasses on the shelf,
Book open at the proper page,
He's turned into 'Himself'.

I hastily replace my shoes,
And as if without a care,
Scan the room for stockings,
There they are, hung on his chair!

Enter! His voice of command,
The one the tenant's dread!
Would ye young ones like a story,
Before ye go tae bed!

A tribe of tired children
Nestle at his feet,
If I could find all of my clothing,
My night would be complete.

'Did I ever tell ye,
the story of the whale?
The great white beast with barnacles,
And a massive thrashing tail.

Granda is waxing lyrical,
As with his words he plays,
And Moby Dick gets harpooned,
He weaves another phrase.

As Ahab meets his nemesis,
Jem's face lights up with glee,
Why are Grannies whalebones,
Hanging on the Christmas tree!

Explain that one, my face is glass!
While his ears are turning red,
That's another story!
Now it's really time for bed!

Shall I spear like a whale
I tell him talk is cheap.
Don't remind me Sassenach!
This old man needs his sleep!

Contemplation

The weans have run riot,
They've broken every rule,
Stolen toffee from the kitchen
It was'nae even cool.

Gifts for everybody,
Even Blue the hound,
She will nae get those antlers off,
Jem stuck them on quite sound!

They've given her a big red nose,
To match her sense of smell,
Mandy glued it in its place,
Held on with caramel.

Brianna and her toolbox,
Roger with his pen,
Ian with his earplugs,
For when Oggie howls again.

To those who are not with us,
We have raised a glass,
To those we miss both kin and friends,
May the absence pass.

Now Time for contemplation,
The old year growing thin,
Short the days, long the nights,
Before the new comes in.

Sitting by the fire,
Wrapped warm in my plaid,
I think back on the times we had,
The good ones and the bad.

I've made a resolution,
Before the year is gone,
I promise I'll forgive ye,
For marrying Lord John.

Ye'll have windows for yer surgery,
And a proper door,
Unless I can'nae help it,
I will nae go to war.

Listen, aggravating Scot,
I make promises I keep,
I won't forget to kiss you,
Each night before we sleep.

I promise that I'll love you,
More than life itself,
Through war and peace and all between
Including lack of wealth.

So, when I wake each morning,
Just promise you'll be there,
Or leave me with a parting kiss,
Or a line of Gaelic prayer.

We need no resolutions,
We are bound by one vow,
If we couldn't find forgiveness,
We would both be dead by now.

If you should ask me up to bed,
    I'd not put up a fight,
I mean to bed, and not to sleep,
After all, it's Christmas night.

Hide And Seek!

Sassenach where are ye?
Are ye outside digging worms
Or are ye in yer surgery
playing wi' ye germs,

Are ye hiding in the kitchen?
Baking tasty treats,
I can'nae smell things burning,
Are they fit enough tae eat?

Are ye in ma study?
Searching for a book,
I ken ye've one for everything
Excepting how tae cook!

Or are ye churning butter,
I can see ye in my mind
I've searched the house from floor to roof,
Yer very hard to find!

If yer are in the bedroom,
Ye are not in the bed,
Did ye climb into the wardrobe,
Are ye hiding there instead.

I think I'll take this blindfold off,
I'm tired of this game.
I've counted tae two hundred,
If to you tis all the same.

I know just where tae find ye,
In life's game of hide and seek,
If I had tae search all through the ridge,
Well, that could take a week.

Yer face when pictured in my mind,
Has often kept me whole,
My hands recall your body,
I have found my heart and soul.

New Years Morn

Rifle on his shoulder,
Hound close by his side,
I watch him walk into the snow,
Not without some pride.

Broad of shoulder, Lean of hip,
Tall and straight as pine,
I wonder at the turn of fate,
The twist that made him mine.

The years have aged his body,
Played tricks upon his soul,
I stitch the wounds and salve the scars,
I pray I keep him whole.

I would not live without him,
I can't list things he's not,
Above all things I know,
He is an aggravating Scot.

A man that I would die for,
As he would die for me,
On New Years morn, he clears his head,
By hunting for our tea.

A man at one with nature
At one with the land.
I know he'll fight for what is right,
As long as he can stand.

All that life has thrown at him
In the struggle to be free.
The good lord In his wisdom
Entrusted him to me

Merry Christmas Sassenachs

Merry Christmas one and all!
Have you trimmed your trees?
Does Jamie dangle from each branch,
Exhibiting his knees?

Christmas is upon us,
Not many days to go,
Another landmark in the drought,
I wonder, will it snow?

There is movement up in Glasgow,
Sam has been to find his kit!
Does he have a coat of blue,
I wonder, will it fit!

Meanwhile, all around the globe,
We wait, with hands unsteady,
Transported back tae Scotland,
Remotes at the ready!

This family will gather,
A great Outlandish Clan,
Poised as we anticipate,
Half a season in the can

But put down your obsession,
As you raise your glass,
Think of those who went before!
Don't let that feeling pass,

Here's to peace across the world,
Let the fighting end,
Take the hand that's offered,
Call your neighbour, friend.

If words could stop the fighting?
We should all pick up a pen,
Write the secret formula,
Heal the world again.

Humanity and kindness
These are Gifts we can afford,
Spread a little joy today!
With words instead of Swords

A Plan For All Season

I hear wheels grinding,
Cogs starting to turn.
Five days and the drought will end,
What then will we learn.

The Frasers are in Scotland,
The ship has docked at last,
There is unfinished business
Things to bury from the past.

Family reunited,
Happiness and relief
A brother will depart this world,
A sister worn with grief.

The power of modern medicine,
Even aided by Claire's skills,
Cannot cure this illness,
Consumption always kills.

A son returns to find his love,
Far across the sea.
A deal done with a lassie
A man at last set free.

A ship will meet a watery grave,
All hands feared lost,
Desperate times, and measures,
The Frasers count the cost.

Ian makes a memory
Before he makes old bones,
The grief he bears is twenty fold,
A hundredweight of stones.

A storm across an ocean
Caused her ship to sink!
Now through a bottle darkly,
A widow turns to drink.

A good friend mourns a fantasy,
His grief as real as day,
Two bodies seeking solace,
Both hearts bleeding with dismay.

Unforgiven carnal knowledge,
A traveller not dead,
A man returns, his ardour burns
Queue the potting shed!

Will there be peace and harmony,
An answer to our prayers,
Hello goodbye, William meets
His father on the stairs.

Through the glass of darkness
Ian faces life,
Ye don't get used tae killing men,
And he has a Quaker for a wife.

A generals resignation,
While his wife bleeds in the mud,
Written on a runners back,
Signed in his hearts own blood.

A hundred thousand angels
Will heal and build life's bridge,
And with a surgeons skill and Roquefort cheese,
We shall head back to the ridge.

Un unexpected twist of plot,
We are left in suspense,
Why is Raymond sorry?
This Faith plot is quite tense.

Now we wait for season eight,
How will things pan out.
All we can do is speculate
To get us through the drought.

Copyright

ISBN: 9798303250369

Other work by the author

The Author has also written a series of books of poetry based on the Outlander Television Series:

Unofficial Droughtlander Relief.
The Droughtlander Progress.
Totally Obsessed.
Fireside Stories.
Je Suis Prest.
Après Le Deluge
Dragonflies of Summer
Semper in Aeternum
Sia air Ochd
Intervallaqua
Facing the Storm
The Blue Vase

Mille Basia Volume 1
Mille Basia Volume 2
Mille Basia Volume 3 part 1.

Ginger like Biscuits - the adventures of a Welsh Mountain Pony. – a short book written for young teenaged horse enthusiasts.

An Arrow Through Time – my debut full length novel, the first of a Trilogy set in Wales.
Bullets Through the Mist – The second book in The Meredith Trilogy

Cassandra's Web – the story of a family torn apart by murder and institutional corruption.

All are published through Amazon.
Or sold through the authors Etsy Shop
poemsandthings.

Email: authormaggiej@gmail.com

Printed in Great Britain
by Amazon